Wendigo Psychosis

A. E. McClish

Chapter 1

She held her gun steady, pointing directly at my chest.

"Look, I'm not going to hurt you," I said slowly, both hands held up to emphasize my words. "I just want to talk."

"Like Hell," the woman snarled. She held her gun firmly, but her hands were shaking and she was… crying? "You bastards tore my daughter apart, and *ate her*."

Oh. That explained the hostility. But why hadn't she shot me yet, if she despised Wendigos so much? I thought for a moment, glancing around and counting my downed dogs. One, two, three…. And how many shots had she missed? Her gun was empty.

She was bluffing.

"Look," I said, making no move toward her. "*I* didn't do any of that. If you haven't noticed, I am a mostly rational specimen of monstrously mutated humanity. You don't need to shoot me."

"Rational?! None of you are rational. You're starving monsters only looking for the next innocent person you can eat."

I tilted my head in a 'sort of' manner of agreement, my hands still raised placatingly. "Most, yes, and I will admit that I am *very* hungry, but if I haven't eaten you yet, you can be pretty sure I won't in the next ten minutes."

I saw a flicker of doubt in her eyes, then a hardening of her expression. Right, *her* life probably didn't matter as much as her daughter's death. I thought for a moment that she was going to rush and attack me, regardless of her empty gun.

"You couldn't fight me off even if I did want to eat you," I added quickly, "not with an empty gun."

She faltered, her hands finally lowering just a bit. Her expression shifted to hopelessness in the face of something she knew she wouldn't be able to change, or even avenge.

"I can help you, you know," I said calmly, still making no move toward her. "Find the ones who did it, that is. I can help you get revenge on the ones who killed her."

My words were met with a frown. "Why?"

"Because I find the lack of control in my brethren to be rather… nauseating."

"A Wendigo with a conscience?"

"If you want to call it that."

"Why me?"

Because she had information no one else I could get to had. "Because otherwise you'll try and hunt me down as a local menace, and I would rather not be bothered."

"What's to say I won't kill you as soon as we've dealt with those other bastards?"

I shrugged. "Eh, that's your choice. After a fight like that, you might have to." I *might* be too hungry to control myself.

She grunted, finally lowering the gun. "You swear you're gonna take me to the ones who killed my daughter?"

"It'll take some research to figure out a way to get to them, but yeah, I'll help you get revenge for your daughter."

"And what do you get in return? I'm not stupid enough to believe you're just doing this out of the good of your frozen heart."

I smiled, lowering my hands. "It won't be much. I need help getting some information I can't reach."

Evidently the sight of my smile, tight grayish skin stretched across too-sharp teeth, wasn't terribly reassuring, because she paled for a moment before steeling herself and nodding.

"Glad that's settled," I said. "Now, if you don't mind, I need to go adopt a new dog and eat, before I lose control of myself. I'll contact you in the next... twenty-four hours or so, and we can settle on an actual agreement."

"Eat?" she repeated, raising a brow, her gaze hardening again. "The dog?"

"What? No, the dog's for companionship, since you shot these three. Dog flesh doesn't sate the hunger, anyway." Not that *anything* did for very long. "I'll find someone already dead or dying, don't worry. There are plenty of them."

It wasn't wise for one of my kind to walk the streets in daylight, or at any time there were *normal* humans around. They tended to panic or react violently to a Wendigo's presence, and while individually they didn't pose much of a threat, in a mob they were more than capable of handling us.

The ironic thing was, we were, every one of us, once one of them. But that didn't matter. We were their predators now, and humans were our prey.

I took back-streets and alleys as I traveled through the city. The weather was cold. It often was these days, except during the very height of summer, and even then the temperatures weren't much more than warm. A light snow was falling, helping to limit vision just a bit. I didn't mind the cold, or the snow. I barely felt the cold, and the snow obscured me from view.

The confrontation with Amica left me ravenous. I was always hungry, but after activity like that, chasing someone down and dodging bullets, that hunger rose to a ravening, barely-controlled level. Another reason to avoid the main streets. The smell of so many warm, living, human bodies could shatter my self-control.

Don't get me wrong, I'm not a poor, tortured, angst-ridden monster fighting against my nature for the sake of my lost humanity. I'm just more practical than most of my brethren. Losing control and eating humans in public was a wonderful way to get yourself killed. I liked living. I wanted to keep doing so.

The snow dampened sound, but not so much that I didn't hear the coughing coming from an alley as I passed.

I paused, listening closely. Moving deliberately to avoid crunching the snow, I stalked down the alley, toward the source of the sound.

There was an old man there, caught in a rather violent coughing fit. It was a fairly common sight. Poor Normals would turn out their elders, freeing up their own meager resources and hopefully appeasing the Wendigos lurking outside.

I didn't mind. It kept my hunger under control and kept me from having to hunt down healthy Normals. Although it did seem a little hypocritical that they called me a monster, then turned around and turned out their own like that.

The old man got over his coughing fit, wheezing a bit as he tried to catch his breath.

4

I stopped trying to be quiet and simply walked toward him. He wasn't going to run. He spotted me, starting with surprise and fear. Spurred on by his helplessness, I stopped holding back my hunger and rushed forward.

The hunger never really goes away. That's our curse. The prevailing theory was that it was a chemical drive, that our brains were constantly emitting a hunger signal and never a satiated. I had seen Wendigos in such a frenzy of hunger that they literally ate until their stomach burst. Usually that only occurred after an extended period of starvation, but it did happen.

The hunger does quiet to a tolerable level, but only with human flesh. Meat from other creatures could take away the worst of the drive, but not nearly so much as human, and a diet only of other meat would lead a Wendigo to a slow decline into hunger insanity. That was a fate I wouldn't wish on anyone.

Blood remained caked under my fingernails, but I did manage to otherwise get myself cleaned up using the mostly-undisturbed snow surrounding me.

My next task was to find a new dog. Dogs made excellent companions. Loyal, trainable, and wonderful hunters, they made life much easier. I had been rather fond of the three Amica had killed, but I couldn't spare the time to mourn them. A new dog would help me maintain my territory and my hunting grounds.

I had an understanding with a few local animal shelters. Over the past several years, as the weather turned perpetually colder and life became harder, such places found themselves increasingly overrun, with ever-fewer resources to care for the animals they acquired. There were a few in the city that would allow me to come by every now and then and adopt a few dogs. The Normals running the shelters obviously didn't *like* me, but I brought the dogs back to say hello often enough that I had convinced them that I didn't just *eat* the canines as soon as I adopted them.

Unfortunately, even if I didn't eat them, most of my dogs didn't live more than a year or two at most, and more often only lived a couple of months. It was a hard life. There were angry mothers seeking revenge for their daughters that might shoot them. But, I provided for them the best I could, and they weren't *unhappy* while they were with me. In fact, they were better cared for with me than they would be at the under-supplied animal shelters.

Once I finished with that, I would go meet with Amica. I knew where she lived; I had been keeping track of her, and a few other people, for years. I needed to identify someone who could help me find my brother, and so far, Amica was my best bet.

I wasn't involved in her daughter's death. That had been a pack of Wendigos whose territory was near mine and encompassed Amica's house and her daughter's school. Their attack had actually been fairly big news; it was the first time such a large group of Wendigos had been witnessed working together. It was a bold attack, and resulted in quite a few deaths. Most of the deaths had been Normals, and mostly children at that. Apparently that pack had a liking for tender flesh. There were a few other schools in their territory, and over time, none of them had gone un-attacked.

Personally, I thought it was stupid to go after children. Those children hadn't done anything, and killing so many of them would undermine the breeding population and bring undue attention to yourself. Despite a Wendigo's superior strength, stamina, and constitution, we *could* still be killed, and we needed the Normals for our own survival.

I paused outside the animal shelter, turning and looking along the street in either direction. This part of the city was never busy at this time of the day, and there didn't seem to be anyone about. Good. I didn't really want to deal with some suburban mom getting her son a puppy while I was in there.

Walking in, I smiled at the receptionist, who visibly blanched at my expression. I wasn't surprised. A Wendigo's smile isn't exactly reassuring.

"Don't worry," I said, "I'm not here to eat anyone. I have an agreement with your boss. Is Mrs. Blanchette in?"

The receptionist stared at me for several long moments, and I was starting to wonder if I had put her in a permanent freeze state when she finally nodded slowly and picked up her phone. She entered a number, barely daring to look away from me. I leaned against the wall, waiting.

"Mrs. Blanchette?" the receptionist said, her voice shaking. "There's a… a Wen… a Wendigo here. He says he has an agreement with you?"

She was silent for a moment, then addressed me. "Are you Jason?" she asked.
I nodded.

"Yes, it's Jason," she said into the phone. She nodded at something the other person said, then hung up. "Ok," she said to me, "you can, uh, go back."

Standing and moving to a door beside her desk, she unlocked it, then took several steps back as I approached, nodded at her pleasantly, and went through to the back of the shelter.

The back smelled strongly of animal. Even to a Normal's nose it would be unpleasant, but to me it was nearly overwhelming. I likely wouldn't be here long, though, and could tolerate it for as long as I needed to.

I walked down the hallway, past side rooms lined with cages of smaller animals, to the back, where there were larger rooms lined with kennels. A few dogs barked as I passed, but most of them simply cowered.

I was met in the back by a short woman. Her medium-brown hair went down to her chin, and was styled to curl under in a little bob. She wore an over-sized green t-shirt and jeans, both of which were stained by long interaction with animals.

"Jason," she greeted me, nodding. Her gaze was locked on me, not leaving me for a second. She didn't trust me, which was only reasonable.

"Katelyn," I returned. "You're looking well."

"You're not," she replied. "Have you been getting in fights again?"

Had I been killing people, she meant.

"Only the one, and she's still alive. I'm meeting her later, actually, to discuss some business. She.... also shot my dogs."

The woman snorted. "Should have put a bullet in you while she was at it, maybe teach you to be a bit more careful with your *companions*."

"That's not fair," I replied. "I take good care of my dogs."

"Until they die."

"We all die."

She huffed again, and turned away, starting down the row of kennels. I followed.

"We have a few dogs that may suit you," she said. "I haven't been able to adopt them out due to temperament, but you seem to have a way with dogs, so they may like you."

I nodded along with her words, observing the kennels as we passed. The dogs back here were mostly larger breeds, and that was what I always went for. A small, yappy dog wouldn't survive two days living with me.

We stopped at the last set of kennels, perpendicular to the rest, blocking in the end of the row. In the kennel on the left was a large black mutt. He looked like he was part German Shepherd, and probably had some sort of bulldog breed mixed in as well. He looked solid, and long-furred enough to survive cold weather. The kennel on the right held what looked suspiciously like a wolf-mix. She was dark gray, with coldly intelligent eyes that followed my movements. I looked at them both for a moment, and they looked back at me. "I think they'll do," I told Katelyn. "Have you been able to do anything with them yet?"

"Just basic vetting. They've both been fixed, and we made sure they had some basic shots."

"Good. That'll be a few less things for me to have to worry about."

I approached the black male, and he lifted his head, posturing, a low half-growl rumbling in his throat. I gently met his gaze and didn't back away. After several moments, he glanced away, lowering his head a bit. I changed to a relaxed stance and told him what a good boy he was in a pleasant voice.

He seemed uncertain, but wagged the very tip of his tail just a bit.

I repeated the same with the female, though it took her longer to calm down and respond to praise. I nodded to Katelyn, who unlocked their kennels. We opened the doors, and as each of the dogs came rushing out, I snapped my fingers. They stopped and looked at me, surprised. I nodded and gave each of them a pat on the head.

Turning, I saw Katelyn watching the dogs warily, looking from them to me. She saw me watching and cleared her throat. "I still haven't found out how you get them to listen so quickly," she said, and turned, heading back to the front.

I followed. "They respond more to body language and tone than actual words," I replied, "and they see me as more similar to them than to a human, which makes most of them curious and willing to listen."

"Hmm. Just take them and go. I don't want any trouble here."

"Of course not," I agreed amicably. I smiled toothily and nodded at her as I left, shooting the receptionist a smile as well. She didn't move from where she sat frozen at her desk while I went through the reception area.

My new companions and I headed out into the snowy evening. The light snow had become thicker, further obscuring vision with large, heavy flakes. The pile-up of snow would make transportation through the city difficult for many people, which would make hunting good for some of the more opportunistic Wendigos.

Glancing at the two dogs and calling for them to follow, I started to lope through the few inches of snow, back toward my house. I would go see Amica in a few hours, but for now I was going to get to know these two. They needed names.

Chapter 2

Shadow and Ash followed me through the city, two silent shadows flanking me, partly obscured by the falling snow. We had been travelling for nearly twenty minutes, alone in the snow-bound city.

We were approaching my house, one in a row of old, decrepit buildings in what was once a moderately-bad neighborhood. Now it was an empty one, except for me and the wild-life, most of which avoided me.

Much of the neighborhood moved South when the climate grew cold, and the rest left when I established the center of my territory here. I would have been fine with them staying, it gave the area a sense of "normalcy" and helped me avoid unwanted attention from government or scientific authorities, but apparently the residents weren't comfortable with a Wendigo living next door.

The two dogs were hesitant about coming inside with me, but after some encouragement, they cautiously slipped inside after me. I shut the door and locked it behind us, though a dog-flap set into it would allow them to go out if they really wanted to.

There wasn't much light filtering in from what lingered outside, so I lit a few candles around the main room. The electricity had been shut off a few years prior, though I wasn't particularly bothered. The cold didn't affect me as it did Normal humans, so long as I took care not to freeze entirely.

While the dogs sniffed around, getting to know the place, I went upstairs to retrieve my own gun and several rounds of ammunition. I hadn't wanted to carry it the first time I met Amica, not wanting to give the entirely wrong impression. Just being a Wendigo was bad enough, as evidenced by three dead dogs.

I gathered up a few other supplies, stowing them all in an old military backpack, the olive-colored canvas faded with age. Shouldering that, I went back downstairs, whistling for the dogs. They didn't come right away, and I whistled again. They came this time, curious, and I praised them for responding.

With them following, I headed back out into the snowy evening.

Amica's house was quite a trek from mine. It was in a different part of the city, in the territory of the pack who had killed her daughter. I didn't want to be spotted moving through it. They probably wouldn't harm me if they did see me; most Wendigos were alright with each other crossing territory lines... so long as there was no *hunting* in the other's territory. I wasn't hunting, but I didn't want to make the pack think that I was up to something.

I kept my eyes peeled as I moved, taking care to step quietly. Shadow and Ash followed my lead, scenting the air and ground as we moved. It must be nice for them to be out of the kennel. We moved slowly for the final mile, and it was nearly nine in the evening by the time we made it to Amica's house.

She lived in a suburban part of the city, outside the central limits, with nice houses and, at one point in time, nicely-manicured lawns. Now, the buildings had a nearly ghostly quality, sitting sentinel in fields of snow with brightly-lit windows staring out into the darkness.

I avoided the patches of light, and the dogs did the same. It would be best not to alarm the Normal humans living here.

Finally reaching the proper house, I stepped up to the door, Shadow and Ash coming up to flank me, and knocked.

It was several moments before someone answered. I waited patiently, unbothered by the snowflakes accumulating on my shoulders and head.

Finally, the door cracked open, and Amica peeked through the gap. She yelped, which made Ash snarl and lunge toward her and the door, which Amica slammed shut just before the dog hit it. I calmed Ash, getting her to sit beside me before I knocked on the door again.

It opened very slowly. "I didn't think you were actually serious," she said, regarding the dogs cautiously. They watched her closely, probably wondering whether she was dangerous or not.

She didn't let me in yet, just watching, deliberating. "You *will* help me avenge my daughter?" she asked, finally.

"That is what I offered," I replied smoothly.

Amica humphed and stepped aside, gesturing me in. I went in. The dogs didn't want to follow at first, but after a moment of coaxing, they came in with me.

Amica kept her tightly-curled hair cut short enough to never get in the way, and her dark brown skin served her well if traveling at night. I knew for a fact that she had conducted more than one investigation in the hours after curfew, managing to avoid detection by patrolling Enforcers. She was a brave woman, and clever. Just more reason to try and convince her to help me.

"I told you that I would help you track down the pack who killed her," I repeated, standing in her living room. "I'm not going to just lie about something like that."

She eyed me like one would a feral animal, although most feral animals would rather run and avoid humans than engage. One that was starving, though... they would attack nearly anything if they thought they could take it down. I met her gaze. Good thing I wasn't very hungry.

After a moment, she looked away. "You never did say what you're getting out of this," she snapped. "Is it their territory you want? Better hunting grounds?"

I shook my head. "My territory is just fine, I don't need a larger one. No..." I frowned, regarding her seriously. "I want something that, as far as I've been able to find out, you're my best chance of getting. You were a scientist before your daughter was killed, weren't you? You might have access to information I'm looking for."

She raised a brow, and I noticed the large chef's knife sitting behind her on the kitchen counter, her hand conveniently close to it. "Do I?" she asked. "It must be some pretty important information if a Wendigo's willing to come to me for it. Are you familiar with my work, or do you just need any scientist?"

I nodded. "I'm familiar. I think you may be able to get me into a place with information on what happened to my brother. I will help you avenge your daughter, and then you will help me find *him*."

"And if I don't?"

"Then I will tear out your liver and eat it in front of you as you die."

Her lips parted a bit into a snarl, her hand reaching back for the knife. The dogs stood, the fur on their backs rising a bit as they sensed her hostility.

I sighed. "I'm joking. Look, I didn't make contact with you in order to eat you. I came to make a reasonable deal between two rational beings. Will you agree, or am I wasting my time?"

I didn't bother holding a hand out for her to shake. I had a feeling she wouldn't want physical contact.

After a long moment, Amica relaxed a bit. "Never knew a *rational* Wendigo... Fine. I'll agree to it. But if I see any treachery coming from you, I *will* kill you. And your dogs."

"The dogs haven't done anything to you," I replied, smiling. I left the teeth out of it. It was supposed to be a friendly smile. I was being friendly.

I would rather avoid her killing my dogs again.

"I will not harm you so long as we are working together," I reiterated one more time, trying to make sure she got it. She gave me a still-skeptical look, then turned and seated herself on a couch by a coffee table strewn with papers.

"So, where are these bastards staying?" she asked.

I crouched down across the table from her, looking over the notes she had written. I didn't know exactly where their lair was, but I knew it would be within their territory. That would be a place to start.

And it looked like she had been busy in the past several years, pulling together information on the pack's movements and activity.

"Why don't you tell me?" I suggested, gesturing at the papers. "You're the one with all the information."

"I thought you would know where they are?" she asked, frowning.

I shook my head. "Just the range of their territory. I don't come this far into it often." Usually just to locate Amica's house. *She* was what I was interested in in this part of the city, after all.

Amica's frown deepened. "So you have no idea where they are?"

"Well, I have *some* idea. I mean, they have to be within their territory, which is only so many miles across. And it would be somewhere secure, somewhere centralized, so they can get to anywhere within their territory quickly, ideally somewhere where they can keep track of local goings-on."

"So... a tall building?"

"Not necessarily, but it will at least be a place where they can set up some sort of camera or radio system. Don't underestimate the usefulness of monitoring radio frequencies; you Normals have all sorts of clandestine channels on there. I'm sure the government isn't happy about that."

"Maybe if the government wasn't so Orwellian, those channels wouldn't have to exist." She looked down at her papers, shifting a few from one stack to another.

I watched her riffle through the papers, noting that the way she sat brought to view a bulge at one of her hips, under her shirt but, presumably, connected to her belt. A gun. So, she had been prepared to kill me when I showed up, if I posed a threat. I was kind of surprised she hadn't used it on Ash when she first answered the door.

After a few moments of shuffling, Amica pulled out a couple papers and slid them my way. "What about one of these places?"

I looked them over. Each paper had a profile of a location, and a small map pointing out where in the city it was. GPS had become less useful over the past few years, as the only legal units were used by the government to track down… dissidents. As if Normals didn't have enough problems with Wendigos, they had to keep killing each other as well. One would think that, between Wendigos and the cold, they would be sick of dying. In any case, printed maps had become much more popular, and these bits were likely copied from a larger map of the entire city.

The first paper was of a park, set near the center of the pack's territory. It wasn't a huge space, just a flat, grassy area with a few walking trails, a pond, and a few stands of trees. I would be willing to bet it was a lot wilder now than it used to be, though. Maintenance of parks was a low priority. There was an event pavilion and building toward the center of the park that looked like it might be a suitable base of operations for one Wendigo, though less suitable for a pack.

The other paper contained a profile of a building a few blocks from the park, still near the center of the territory. It was a rather tall building for this part of the city, leering over its neighbors by a few floors. According to the profile, the building had been abandoned for a few years, ever since the company that owned it went out of business back when the weather got colder. They had been a decently-popular swimming pool company, but weren't exactly in-demand anymore.

I was rather surprised the building hadn't been bought by some other business, but maybe, with the rise of Wendigo activity around the same time, they hadn't been able to find any buyers and had just let it sit empty.

Or maybe the people who owned it were dead, and thus couldn't use it or sell it.

"Either of these locations would be possible," I said. I placed a finger down on the small map pointing out the abandoned business building. "I think this one is more likely. They can keep watch from the top, it'll be labyrinthian enough to avoid any government raids, and it'll honestly just be more comfortable. We should case that one out first."

She took the paper back, looking over it. "It almost seems obvious," she commented sourly, likely annoyed that she hadn't picked out that location on her own previously.

I shrugged. "It's only a potential. It's likely they have multiple base locations, and move around every few months or so. The government doesn't like *packs*. They pose too much of a threat for the Normals."

Amica scowled at me. "But single Wendigos are fine?"

I shrugged. "The threat of an individual Wendigo holding a particular territory is enough to keep people there from opposing the government's restrictions. It's a balancing game. They don't like us, but that doesn't mean they won't use us."

I tapped on the paper still in her hand. "*This* is a potential location, but likely only one of dozens of empty buildings in the general area, and I doubt you've covered them *all* in your profiles."

"You would be surprised," she retorted. "I see a lot of the area on the job. I've had plenty of time to case the neighborhoods."

"Ahh, yes," I said, "you've taken up being some sort of private investigator, right? Are you State sanctioned?"

"My activities are allowed," she replied, giving me a stern look.

"But not *condoned*?" I specified. "Do you have a license?"

Her look sharpened into a glare, and she shook her head.

I leaned forward a bit, toward her. It seemed odd that she would be allowed to work without a license. "Then what *do* you have?"

"I have more experience putting together pieces of data than most official detectives," she stated, not leaning away from me. "And I have a fully-functioning lab."

"A lab," I repeated.

"A biology lab," she specified.

"Ahh." I leaned back, rocking back on my heels and standing. "So you're allowed to continue your activities because you can solve enough cases via basic DNA analysis to keep the locals calm, even though they have a large pack of Wendigos living just next door." I started walking around the room absently, thinking about that set-up.

"That's interesting, you know," I mused. "Rather than bring in a squad to wipe out the pack, the government's going the circuitous route and letting them live... I wonder why."

"I don't care why the government's letting them live," Amica snapped. "*I'm* going to take them down, and make them pay for what they did to my daughter. If I have to go against the government to do it, I *don't care*."

I chuckled. The sound was unpleasant even to my ears. I guess I just didn't laugh enough to be good at it. "That's a good way to end up dead," I said, "unless you go about your revenge smarter than both the pack and the government. You know... I'm rather surprised you haven't gone after them on your own before now."

20

She stared at me angrily for a long moment, then looked away, the anger draining. She shrugged. "There never seemed to be a good opportunity. I've been gathering information, preparing, seeking them out, but every time I think I get close, they aren't there. And there's always more preparation to do."

I nodded. "It's probably good that you *haven't* confronted them."

"You think I can't take them down?"

"Yes." I regarded her, looking her up and down. "I am a single Wendigo. I can run faster than you," I began ticking each point on my fingers, "I'm stronger, I can hear, see, and smell better. Last time, you killed my dogs, but I wasn't trying to hunt you down. If I had wanted to kill you, I could have. How do you think you would fare against half a dozen or more of my kind, even if you are smarter by half than I am?"

"Then it's a good thing I have you along, isn't it," she snapped back, crossing her arms and standing. "We'll need to case the place, make sure they're there. If they are, we'll need to know the entrances and exits, and their patterns of movement."

I nodded agreement. "And," I added, "we'll have to avoid detection. *That* will be the hard part. With as many of them as there are, the odds are good that we'll be discovered before we even get close to their hideout."

Amica scowled. "I'm aware of that problem."

Nodding again, I started toward the door. "Why don't you sleep on it. I'm going to consider the matter myself, and will return when I have something figured out. I know where to find you." I whistled to the dogs, who stood and followed me as I started toward the door.

"You're just *leaving*?" Amica asked.

"It would be best for me not to remain in the pack's territory for too long. It may draw attention." I paused, turned, and picked up a pen and piece of paper from the coffee table. Quickly, I jotted down the address of my own lair. "You can find me here if you need to."

I handed the paper to her, and left.

Chapter 3

I returned to my own territory, but not to my house. I needed to think for awhile. Loping through the darkness, I was obscured by the falling snow, the two dogs pacing along beside and behind me. They didn't seem to mind the snow, and I was sure the exercise was welcome after being locked up in the animal shelter.

I had already known that Amica had taken up something of a PI career. She didn't take many jobs, but the ones she did I knew she was paid well for. She was stubborn and smart, a good combination for such work. The connection between her being allowed to continue those activities, and the continuation of the large pack whose territory she lived in, though, was something I hadn't thought of before. It was.... not comforting.

The government didn't take kindly to people nosing into business it considered its own. Just as they didn't like enough Wendigo activity to panic (or wipe out) their populous, they didn't like anyone *within* that populous stirring up too much trouble. Someone investigating the troubles and complaints of those who felt that the government perhaps wasn't the best thing for the people could stir up a lot of trouble.

It was a good thing for me that the government mostly left solitary Wendigos alone. I could essentially do what I wanted without worry of curfews, patrols, raids, and the other various limitations imposed on the Normals in the name of "safety," so long as I didn't interfere too much with those patrols.

The sound of growling brought me out of my thoughts, and I halted just before I loped out of an alley into a wider street. Both dogs had stopped, illuminated by light that came from the street ahead. Their hackles were up, and they were both growling fiercely, but they didn't move forward. Each had one ear turned toward me, waiting to see what I was going to do. I was glad that they were already willing to take such cues from me.

I stepped to the side of the alley and the dogs followed me, backing out of the light.

In the street were two large military trucks, several people in the back of each. They were dressed in the current civilian-military style: easily-distinguishable, reinforced, black clothing. These people were Enforcers, the ones who made sure people obeyed curfew, among other laws.

Of course, there weren't many citizens in the area who would willingly go out after curfew with me around, but there were still some homeless holed up in the hidden areas of the neighborhoods, and occasionally one or two would get unlucky and be caught where they shouldn't be.

That seemed to be the case here. Several of the Enforcers had jumped down from their vehicles and surrounded some poor wretch, the scene brightly lit by headlights.

The smell of blood reached me, and I shifted restlessly, stomach growling as fierce hunger was triggered by the scent. I had eaten earlier, sure, but I was still hungry. I was always hungry.

They were taking it in turns to kick the struggling figure on the ground. Occasionally I would catch glimpses of light

reflected from metal spikes on the bottoms of their boots. The
spikes were supposedly for better grip on ice, and while they
did help with that, they had... other uses as well.

The smell of blood grew stronger.

It was difficult to hold myself back. I needed to eat,
needed to assuage the relentless gnawing emptiness of my
stomach. I nearly stepped forward, into the light, but managed
to stop myself.

I had seen traps before, set for Wendigos. Traps where
Enforcers would lure them out with the scent of blood and a
helpless victim, and then shoot until the Wendigo was nothing
but a pulpy mass of flesh. I didn't know if this was a trap or not,
but I didn't want to take that chance.

Even if it was taking every single ounce of self-control I
had not to rush them all, not to tear them apart, sate myself on
their blood and flesh until that terrible hunger abated for a few
more hours.

I closed my eyes and took a deep breath through my
mouth. No. Wait, I told myself. They would leave the poor
wretch lying in the street, and then I could claim the body once
they had gone.

It was impossible to change what I was, but I did think of
myself as a civil monster. Leaving someone's body lying in the
middle of the street was, put simply, barbaric. I would at least
put the body to use; give them some sort of continuation as fuel
for myself, and a discreet disposal out of the way of prying eyes.

After what seemed a lifetime, the victim stopped moving.
The Enforcers laid a few more kicks on them, then, apparently
satisfied that their point was made, did indeed leave the body

there as they returned to their vehicles. They drove off, one of the vehicles running over an arm of the body lying in the street.

I didn't wait until they were out of sight. My self-control was on its last thread. I *needed* to eat.

I returned home after that, slipping into the dark, barely-warmer-than-outside house that served as my lair. My worries about the government's connection to the pack that killed Amica's daughter were set aside for the night. The dogs followed me upstairs, where we all curled up together on the bed and fell asleep as the first touches of pre-dawn lit the city outside.

Wendigos don't need to sleep as often as humans, but when we do go for a few days without sleep, we sleep very heavily. Anything more than a doze puts us just short of a hibernation state, and given such vulnerability while sleeping, many respond violently if woken early. It was important, then, to have a safe place to sleep, for when dozing a couple times a day wasn't quite enough.

I slept through the early morning hours, and all through the next day. The dogs could leave and return as they desired through the dog-door, though they were just as content to sleep long hours, resting after a large meal. When I awoke, they were both beside me, stirring as I did and regarding me in the darkness. I heard one yawn, and yawned as well, quickly followed by the other dog.

Yawns are contagious no matter what you are.

I wasn't in any particular hurry to get out and about. A peek around a light-blocking curtain on one of the bedroom windows showed me that the snow had stopped, but that it had left what looked like at least six inches coating the world outside. It would make travel a little more difficult.

26

Sorting through my stash of clothes and considering what to wear, I recalled the problem of the previous night. The government appeared to be arranging things in favor of the pack's continued existence. If the government wanted, they could kill every Wendigo in that territory. Instead, they let things be, and let Amica solve some of her neighbors' problems without official licensing, likely to help assuage some of the dissent stirred up by the presence of so many Wendigos.

I knew that by the time I reached her house, Amica would likely be asleep, and I didn't want to be shot for waking her. It wouldn't make sense to go back to her right away, anyway, not without a plan. That left me the entire night to case things out.

My usual garb was almost always shades of gray, or brown if I was feeling colorful. It stood out less in the snowy city landscape, and I wasn't really one for wearing white. It showed too much blood. Tonight, I went with a darker gray, to fit with the shadows of night on snow. I wanted to be as inconspicuous as possible.

I whistled for the dogs as I headed downstairs. They followed eagerly, happy to be getting out again. Together, we headed out into the still darkness.

It must have been just approaching curfew, after dark but not yet enforced. There were a few people around on the streets, but I ignored them, and they avoided me. I was a common-enough sight in the area, even if I tended to avoid the main streets, and most of the Normals knew I wouldn't bother them if they steered clear of me.

Well, except for a few instances when I was *exceptionally* hungry, but that hadn't happened for about a year or so.

Speaking of hunger… My gaze lingered on a young couple hurrying somewhere on the other side of the street. After a moment, I looked away and continued on. No, killing here would just bring undue attention to myself. I had other things to do, and really, my hunger was quite manageable at the moment.

I continued on through the city, returning to the pack's territory, though this time I didn't head toward Amica's house. Instead, I made my way toward the territory's center.

Slowing my pace once I was a few blocks in, I carefully moved forward, paying attention to the shadows and slipping from one to another. It would be less suspicious to move in a non-furtive manner, just in case I *was* seen, but I would much rather just avoid detection altogether.

The dogs picked up on my caution, and became nothing more than shadows behind and beside me, moving as I did through the shadowed city. A few streets retained bright street-lights, and these I avoided, but far more were a patchwork of light and shadow, lit by only a few dim, flickering lamps.

I continued on steadily, the city now silent around me as curfew came and went. It wasn't enforced for Wendigos, part of what made it so effective in getting the Normals to actually stay in. Anyone caught out after curfew was fair game.

The silence was a boon to my travel, my attention just as much on listening as on keeping my own movement as silent as possible. At one point the rumble of an Enforcer truck sent me slipping back into a darkened alley, watching silently until it had passed and turned a corner out of sight.

I reached the park that had been in Amica's notes a little after eleven. The snow lay in a soft, nearly-unbroken sheet across the expanse, only occasionally marred by the footprints of urban animals. I paused at the edge, looking out over the area from the relative cover of a tree, my gray clothes blending against the darkness of the trunk. My dogs came to sit beside me, sniffing the area excitedly.

I stood there for a few minutes, just watching. There didn't appear to be much moving in the shadowy snow-covered setting. Occasionally I spotted a feral cat or dog, or a scurrying rodent of some kind. Other than that, the park seemed still.

I gestured to the dogs, and they stood. Turning, I began walking around the edge of the park, still moved cautiously to avoid being spotted. Simply traveling through another's territory was one thing. Being caught lurking in the heart of it was another.

Suddenly, Shadow stopped, perking his ears as he listened to some distant noise. Ash followed his example, and I stopped as well, listening carefully with the dogs. There, a commotion, at least a block away.

After several moments of listening, I began moving again, toward the noise. I wanted to get just close enough to hear what was going on. There was a partially-forested part of the park here, a group of trees with decorative, now uncared-for and mostly-dead, plants growing underneath. I moved to set my path through there, using the meager undergrowth to obscure myself.

I went until the patch of trees ended then halted and listened. The sound of the commotion had definitely grown louder. It sounded like several voices, calling and howling and laughing, all together. The Pack. They were likely out hunting, counting on their greater numbers to flush out any potential prey and not caring about the noise they were making. Certainly, they could chase down any Normal who happened to be outside.

I was willing to bet *very* few would be.

The sound grew louder, and I realized they were heading toward me. I crouched down, laying nearly prone in the snow, hoping the dogs would get down as well. It wouldn't do to be caught by a hunting party, Wendigo though I was. There were some who enjoyed the hunt enough to chase down whatever they came across, food or not. And on top of that, with a whole group, I was much less likely to be let off easy for being in their territory. I could reason with or intimidate an individual. A group would urge each other on, each wanting to show off for the others.

No, it would be best *not* to be spotted.

I watched as they came into view, six of them, heading down the street at a steady lope. Their attitudes were jovial, and I guessed that they had already been successful at least once on their hunt.

Thankfully, they were on the far side of the road bordering the park, and none detected my presence as they passed. I waited until they were out of sight and hearing before daring to stand again. I brushed the snow off myself and slipped out of the protection of the trees, followed closely by Shadow and Ash.

Deliberating for a moment, I stood at the edge of the park, looking both ways down the street. What to do next? The pack didn't seem to have come from the park itself, and I had found no indication of Wendigo activity coming from this location. It was time to move on.

Looking up and around, I spotted the tall, abandoned building from the other paper. That was where I was going next. I wouldn't dare venture too close, but I could at least observe from a nearby alley, and that should be enough to tell me whether or not the pack had their base of operations there.

I continued down the street, still avoiding any pools of light. The dogs loped along beside me, quiet and attentive. They seemed to like activity like this, travel with a purpose.

The pack's first kill could be smelled before I saw it. The scents of blood and death hung thickly in the air, and, diverting slightly from my path toward the old office building, I followed the smell. I came upon the remains in the middle of the sidewalk. It looked like the Normal had been dragged from the adjacent alley, judging by the blood splattered and streaked across the snow. There wasn't much more than bones and hair left to whoever this had once been, and scraps of bloody, torn clothing.

I considered moving the body into the alley, covering it with snow properly in at least a little respect for the dead, but if this was the normal way of leaving kills in this territory, the movement of one could raise suspicion.

Ash sniffed at the remains, choosing a bone and gnawing on it for a moment while I oriented myself again toward the office building. Letting Ash bring the bone, as the body would shortly be scattered by scavengers, anyway, I whistled for the dogs to follow as I started down the alley itself.

The alley came out a few blocks down from the office building. This part would be tricky, if the abandoned building was indeed the center of their operations. If they had any sentries on the higher floors, any movement on the street would be easily and quickly spotted, which meant I would have to be very careful.

Of course, most of the pack may have been with that hunting party, leaving only a skeleton watch at the base, or even none at all. I didn't want to bet on that, though. Better to be cautious and alive.

I crossed the street quickly, leaving myself exposed in the open for as little time as possible, and headed toward the building. I was now on the same side of the street as it, and moving along the buildings would keep me at a less-visible angle to anyone keeping watch from above.

The office building loomed over the buildings around it. It would have cast an impressive shadow had it been day, but now it merely sat dark and foreboding against the skyline, a block of more solid shadow against the clouded night.

Our progress was slow. I wanted any movement I made to go unobserved, and if it *was* observed, to be unremarkable. I moved slowly, randomly and with many pauses, presenting anything other than a purposeful approach. Anyone who saw me wouldn't immediately realize what they were seeing, and when they looked back, I would be still and nigh invisible in the dark.

Finally, I drew near the old building. It stood on the corner of an intersection, and I stopped on the far side of the second street bordering it. I didn't dare get any closer than that. Thankfully, one of the businesses on this side had an entrance that was pulled back and to the side from the actual sidewalk, making a shadowed alcove partially blocked from sight. It would be a near-perfect location to wait and watch.

I lowered myself into a hunter's crouch and waited patiently, the dogs lying down on either side of me. For several minutes there was no movement on the street or from the office building. I continued waiting.

After nearly forty-five minutes, I was tempted to move on and discount this location, or at least note it as less-likely to be the pack's current center of operations. I decided to remain just a little longer, though, and after a few more minutes became glad that I did. The pack returned, at a slower pace now, and quieter, apparently sated by a successful hunt.

They approached the building and, one by one, slipped inside as their apparent leader held the door open. She looked around carefully before she, too, went inside, closing the door behind her.

That was that, then. I had them. Or at least, I knew exactly where they were. It would take further preparation to actually infiltrate the location and route them out, but knowing where to look for them was certainly a start. After a few more minutes I stood, stretching my legs for a moment, then whistled quietly for the dogs to follow as I slipped out of my hiding spot. I would have to be even more careful leaving, just in case more of them were now posted on watch duty. I made it nearly a block before a voice hissed out at me from an adjacent alley.

"So what do you think you're doing here, Jason?"

Chapter 4

The dogs started growling as another Wendigo stepped out of the darkness of the alley, approaching me. As she did, I could hear the sound of others approaching, moving to stand behind and around me. It sounded like three of them, plus the first.

"Just out for some late-night Birthday shopping," I replied, smiling at her. It was a toothy smile, just short of outright challenge, but a statement that I wasn't just going to cower down in front of the pack's leader.

She returned my smile with an amused one of her own, shifting the long scar that ran down the left side of her face from her forehead to the base of her cheek. "Oh, please, old friend, we both know that's not what you're doing. Now, why don't you tell us why you're here, at the heart of our territory, and we will afford you the courtesy of not killing you."

"You mean you haven't already figured it out, Rachel?" I replied. "You've always had to know *everything*." I placed on hand on the head of each of my dogs, reassuring them. They stopped growling, though their hackles remained raised.

"I don't need to know *everything*," she replied. "*You're* the one who *insisted* on knowing the whereabouts of someone already dead. I just need to know enough to keep my family here safe." She moved a few steps closer, and I could hear the other three Wendigos moving closer as well, encircling me.

"Now," Rachel continued, "*why* are you here? Are you still looking for your poor, lost brother? You know you won't find him here."

"What I'm doing here isn't your business," I snapped. "I'm just passing through."

She laughed. "Just passing through?! And you just *happen* to sit and rest outside our building for nearly an *hour*, and then leave as soon as the hunting party comes back in? No, no, Jason," she leaned forward, her face near mine as she continued to speak. A strand of dark brown hair fell across her face. "You were casing us out. Did you find out what you wanted?"

I didn't move away from her. "Yes, I found out what I wanted," I stated. "And now, if you don't mind, I am going to go back to my own territory. I hardly pose a threat to you and your pack, Rachel, and you know it."

She leaned back, considering me for a long moment. The other Wendigos shifted restlessly.

"Fine," she said after a long moment. "For old time's sake. But first..." she looked at the other three Wendigos, who awaited her word eagerly, "we really do need to make an example of you. It's poor management of a territory to just let an outsider snoop around as they please. You three, don't kill him, just rough him up."

"What about the dogs?" one of them asked.

The dogs started growling again.

Rachel looked down at the dogs, then back at me. "There's no need to kill them, either. Not tonight. I'll just... pad the odds a bit for us." Pulling a gun from a holster at her hip, she aimed and shot.

I started to lunge forward, but the Wendigo behind me tackled me before I could, knocking both of us to the snowy ground.

I heard a yelp, and saw Shadow fall. Ash, too, yelped, before turning and running away. Apparently she was gun-shy. That was fine with me. Snarling, I struggled against the Wendigo on top of me, maneuvering to get a better position.

Rachel started to turn and walk away, then paused. "Oh, and say hello to that PI friend of yours. Let her know that her last client sends his regrets, but he won't be getting back to her."

That wasn't good. I didn't have time to think about it at the moment, though, as one Wendigo was holding me down while the other two moved to stand over me.

I grunted and snarled as a heavy boot landed a firm kick against my ribs, losing whatever small ground I was gaining against the opponent on top of me. I had managed to turn over, so I was facing him at least, but with the blow to my side I lost any chance of getting back up.

I wasn't a *poor* fighter; in fact, I was stronger and more skilled than many Wendigos, and certainly more rational, but that wasn't helping me against *three* of them, especially not when they already had me on the ground.

A few of my attempts to fight back managed to land, but far more didn't, and after several blows I stopped trying to fight back, instead simply laying still and taking it. The sooner they felt they were finished, the sooner I could check on Shadow and make sure he was going to be ok.

I wasn't sure how long they spent kicking and hitting and biting, but eventually they seemed to grow bored and broke off, leaving me there on the blood-spattered snow. Groaning, I pulled myself upright, moving over to check on Shadow. He had pulled himself a short distance away and was laying down, whimpering. I checked him over and saw that he had only been shot in the foreleg, and that the shot had, thankfully, not broken any bones. I pet him for a moment, reassuring him, and he licked my hand in return, perhaps trying to reassure me in turn.

I stood slowly and painfully, encouraging Shadow to do the same. He didn't want to, but as I started moving away, he brought himself to three legs and limped after me. I didn't move quickly, and I didn't bother trying to hide my movement through the pack's territory. It was too late for that.

Ash was still gone, though I hoped that she would come back now that the coast was clear. Having one able-bodied being on this team would be a good thing, even if I could be reasonably sure that the pack wasn't going to attack again immediately. They had made their point.

I headed straight toward my territory, keenly feeling the myriad of forming bruises and cracked bones where I had been beaten. My hunger was quickly rising to a maddening level by my injuries, and it was all I could do to keep moving forward toward my territory rather than trying to tear my way into a house or apartment by sheer force in order to consume the warm, unsuspecting life within.

After several blocks, I spotted Ash shadowing us, keeping a bit of a distance, but when I stopped and acknowledged her, she came closer. She seemed upset, her head low and tail tucked. I reassured her for a few moments, and after she assured herself that Shadow and I were not mortally wounded, we all moved slowly on.

Finally, we crossed the street that marked the boundary between the pack's territory and my own. As soon as I was past it, I lifted my head, listening as I smelled the air. I was *hungry*, and was finding it increasingly difficult to think about anything else. I released control and hunted the streets after the nearest human I could find.

It was dawn before we finally got back to my house. After coming back to myself, I had stopped long enough to check Shadow's leg before heading back. Thankfully, the bullet had gone all the way through, so I didn't have to go in and remove it.

The way back had been slow. I healed rapidly, but I would still be sore for several days, and with several cracked ribs, I wasn't moving very quickly. I was covered in blood, both my own and not. Shadow was not using his bad leg, and his fur was matted with his own blood, while Ash shadowed us, sometimes ranging ahead protectively.

We slipped into the house thankfully, none of us making it further than the main living-room. I sat on the couch, Ash leaning against my leg. Shadow lay down only a few steps inside the doorway, his bad leg held awkwardly beside him. I would need to take care of that before anything else.

After a few minutes of gathering my resolve, I pushed myself to my feet again and went to retrieve my first aid kit.

The kit was a large toolbox filled with various medical supplies, including bottles of clean water and several less-than-legal drugs. I brought it out to Shadow, who looked at me suspiciously but didn't move. I gave him a shot to numb the pain, and one of antibiotics. Once I was sure the shot of pain meds was starting to kick in, I went about cutting the blood-matted hair from the immediate area around the bullet hole.

After that, I cleaned and dressed the wound, taking any steps I could to keep it from becoming infected and to make sure it healed well.

After I finished with Shadow, I stood and took the kit back to the bathroom, which was really more of a formality than useful. The water lines had frozen and cracked long ago.

My dog seen to, I set about cleaning myself up. There wasn't much chance of infection, as there were very few bacteria that could survive at the temperature a Wendigo's body burned at. Still, it was best for the wounds to be dressed properly, to help them heal more quickly.

The sun was fully up, albeit hidden behind clouds, by the time I finished. Leaving the bathroom a mess for now, I stumbled up the stairs to my bed and collapsed onto it, feeling the acute ache of bruises and broken ribs. The gnawing of hunger was returning to rival that ache. I ignored both of those sensations and tried to do some thinking, but my thoughts slipped away like water. After a few minutes, I gave up and let myself slip in and out of an uneasy doze.

It was dark when I got back up. I groaned as I urged my body back into movement, feeling injured and healing tissues protesting after being unmoved for several hours. I sat on the edge of the bed for a few minutes until I felt like moving again, using the time for some serious thinking.

The pack had known I was there. They also knew about Amica, and knew I had made contact with her. Did someone tip them off? Had I been tailed? *And* Rachel was the leader of the pack, which meant... well, I really wasn't sure what it meant. It had been a few years since we had worked together, and while we knew a lot about each other, that knowledge was now years out of date. She was ruthless and occasionally cruel. She was also *extremely* intelligent, and very well in control of herself.

There was a lot of information to sift through. I tried to focus on what would be most important, but it was difficult to over the gnawing of hunger. Healing really did take a lot of energy.

I pushed the matter of thinking away for the moment and went downstairs. There, I checked on Shadow, who stood to greet me and even put a bit of weight on his injured leg. Neither dog seemed interested in going with me when I headed out, though, and I didn't mind that. They could stay in and rest.

When I returned an hour or so later, my head was much clearer. On the way back I had considered the current circumstances, organizing my problems into a cohesive list. First on that list was Amica. Rachel told me that the pack knew I had spoken to the human, which meant that they may go directly after her. I would need to return, despite the likely kill-on-sight order now up for me in that territory, and warn her. If I could convince her, I would bring her back to my place, where she would be significantly safer.

I couldn't afford to lose her as a potential source of information.

After that... we needed a plan. Of course, were they to notice us making a move, our actions would be seen as requiring further retribution. They may just decide to invade my own territory, and while they had a large territory to hold as it was and couldn't afford the energy to manage a larger one, there was no loss to them in opening my territory up for whatever Wendigo wanted to come in and take it for themselves once I was dead.

I would really rather that not happen. I would have to return to Amica without being seen, and our plan would have to be a *good* one.

That meant going back in daylight, when the streets were busy with Normals, and Wendigos seen on the streets were likely to be shot. It was much less likely that any pack members would be out and about to see me. I just hoped they didn't have Amica's house watched during the day.

Shadow wasn't going to be much good on such a trip with his injured leg, but it would be nice to have at least one of the dogs with me, to help keep watch and provide back-up. I would bring Ash with me, if she could be convinced away from her injured comrade.

For now, though, I had several hours until full daylight. I wasn't quite sure what to do with myself during that time, aside from planning, which I couldn't get far on without Amica's notes and maps of that part of that city.

I sighed and sat on the couch, head tilted back as I contemplated the problem. To get the information I needed from Amica, I had to help her get revenge for her daughter. To do that, I had to take out a pack of Wendigo who far exceeded me in numbers, and who were led by someone just as smart and controlled as myself. Honestly, Rachel was probably smarter *and* stronger than I was.

It was a problem.

I couldn't think of a solution. Eventually, my thoughts drifted and I dozed off, sitting there on the couch. The cost of accelerated healing was fatigue and hunger, and both were hitting me hard. I let myself rest through the night, slipping in and out of sleep. There wasn't much to do until daylight, anyway, so healing was a good enough use of my time.

Waking from a particularly long stretch of sleep, I noted the slant of light through the windows. It was time to head out.

Ash was laying beside Shadow, dozing. She lifted her head to watch me as I stood and stretched. I called her over as I started toward the door. She seemed a little hesitant, but after a moment she stood and followed me out, leaving Shadow behind. He started to stand and follow as well, but I gestured for him to stay and he lay back down, not entirely reluctantly.

I didn't bother taking side streets and alleys. I wanted to get through my territory as quickly as possible, making the most efficient use of my time. Many people gave me nervous looks and stares as I jogged along, some even crossing the street to avoid me. I paid them no mind.

The sun was out, reflecting brightly off the snow. It was rather painful to my dark-sensitive eyes, and a poignant reminder of why I hunted at *night*.

I made it to the edge of my territory with no incident. I could smell Lake Michigan a couple blocks away as always, a helpful cue, and turned, heading south. I slowed then, moving to the side-streets and alleyways as I entered the pack's territory.

It took much longer to reach Amica's house than it had to reach the border of my territory. I didn't go right up to it immediately, tucking myself into a hiding place down the street and watching for any indication that the pack was monitoring the location.

I didn't see anything, though that didn't necessarily mean there wasn't anyone there. They could simply be watching from somewhere I couldn't see from where I crouched.

42

Well, staying where I was wasn't going to get anything done.

Gesturing for Ash to remain where she was, I moved forward, down the street and up to the door of Amica's house. I knocked, and waited.

And waited.

She didn't answer. I knocked once more, waited a few more moments, then tried the door. It was locked. That, at least, was a good sign.

Perhaps she was simply out.

Grimacing at the necessity of remaining in the pack's territory any longer, I moved back to where Ash was sitting, and waited.

Waiting for a quarry requires patience. Wendigos are better with the chase than the stalk; the push of our hunger simply doesn't allow for extended patience. But this wasn't a hunt for the sake of satiating hunger, and I could wait however long it took for Amica to return.

Assuming I wasn't discovered.

And assuming she actually did come back.

I waited for nearly two hours, the sun moving slowly across the sky. Sitting there in the snow, I was glad that the cold didn't bother me, and that Ash had very thick fur.

Finally, I spotted Amica coming down the street. She seemed to be in a hurry, walking briskly toward her house while scanning her surroundings constantly. That was odd.

I scanned the area, looking for anything suspicious, but didn't see anything.

Whistling for Ash to follow, I left my hiding place and moved down the street to intercept Amica as she arrived at her house. She spared me only a surprised glance as I met her at her door, followed by a troubled frown. I followed her inside, and she shut and locked the door behind us.

"They know you've been here," she said.

"I know," I replied, and pointed at the yellowed bruises still visible on my pallid face.

She stared at them for a moment. "When did that happen?"

"About a day and a half ago. The night after we last talked. I went and cased out the pack's territory."

"And they caught you?" she asked drily.

"Obviously. I was left with a warning, and with the information that they already knew about our meetings. I'm pretty sure they killed your last client, too."

Amica nodded at that. "They've been watching me," she stated. "They left a note on my office door to find when I got back from lunch."

I frowned. "Did any of them follow you here?"

"I don't know," she replied. "I didn't see any, but they apparently have some very good trackers."

"Of course they do," I commented drily. How else would they have ambushed me so neatly? "Would you be willing to come back with me?"

She raised a brow at that. "What, back to your house? A human staying with a Wendigo? I should just walk right in and make myself at home and expect nothing bad to happen to me?"

"Yes, actually. If the pack has decided that you've become a liability, any danger you'd be in from me should seem trivial. You *did* decide to allow me to help you get revenge on them, and you can't do that if you stay here and get killed, or if I'm killed coming to talk to you."

She didn't seem happy with those options, but after a moment of thought she relented. "Fine," she said. "Suppose I do go with…"

Amica paused as Ash began growling, the dog's fur standing on end and her ears back as she stared at the door. Something moved past the window outside.

I got a sudden, very bad feeling.

"We need to go," I said. "Now."

"What about my papers?"

"You can't bring them all." I looked around, trying to think through what I knew of the house's layout. I didn't know for certain who or what was outside, just that Ash didn't like them. I would be willing to bet that both the front and back doors were being covered, which ruled out both of those as exits.

"I'm not leaving my research here for them to take!" Amica stated, turning and hurrying up the stairs.

I made to grab her and hold her back, but I missed and she continued on, wasting precious time with papers that… well, that would probably prove very useful. Growling to myself in frustration, I set Ash to watch the door as I moved through the rest of the downstairs, looking over the windows for the best potential escape route.

Any on the same sides of the house as the doors were out. Any sealed shut were out. That left… I found that the bathroom window was unsealed, possibly for just such a circumstance as this. It was openable and big enough to climb through. It did have a screen, but that could be easily remedied. There were large, densely-foliaged pine trees outside it as well. Perfect.

I turned at the sound of footsteps, tensing in preparation of handling whatever was coming in, but it was just Amica, a backpack slung over her shoulders.

"Come on," she said, acting far more urgently than she had a few minutes ago. "We need to get moving quickly."

"I tried to tell you that," I growled.

She stepped past me, pulling a folding knife from a side pocket of the backpack and slicing the screen. As she went through, I caught sense of a worrying smell. Smoke. Were they trying to burn us out?

I pushed that thought aside. No matter, we were leaving anyway. I whistled for Ash, then followed Amica through the window. My dog appeared and followed close behind us, still quietly growling uneasily.

We paused beneath the down-hanging pine branches. It wasn't roomy, but there was enough space for us to crouch under concealment. It was still light out, the sun shining brightly. That, at least, was a disadvantage to any Wendigos who may be getting set to attack. Of course, it was also a disadvantage to myself, who was just as glare-blinded as any other Wendigo would be.

Amica pointed through a gap in the branches, through which we could see down the street. Nearly a block away were two Enforcer trucks. There were a few Enforcers standing near the trucks, but far fewer than I knew the vehicles could hold. The rest must be surrounding the house.

"They stopped far enough away that we couldn't hear the trucks," I murmured to Amica. This was good and bad news. Enforcers meant we were working with humans, and humans

46

were usually easy to shake. Unfortunately, it also meant that we were dealing with more heavily-armed individuals than most Wendigos, and in higher numbers. No amount of rapid healing could overcome a well-placed gunshot.

The smell of smoke was becoming sharper, and as I sat there listening, I could hear the crunch of several pairs of boots on the snow.

"They're going to break into the house," I whispered. "When they do, we run."

Amica nodded, readying herself to run as soon as commotion began. She had an odd expression on her face, both grim and pleased. I glanced from her to the house, realizing that the smell of smoke must be her doing. She had likely set whatever papers she couldn't carry with her on fire.

At that moment, I heard two doors being forced open, both front and back. Amica and I were off, myself just a fraction of a second before her. Ash flanked us, staying close.

We moved parallel to the street for several paces, then turned and dashed away from it, toward the houses behind the ones in Amica's row. Behind us, there were shouts as our movement was spotted.

The sound of several gunshots nearly deafened me as we ran, a few bullets whizzing uncomfortably close. We managed to make the next row of houses, and then the next street.

I pointed for us to turn, and we went down the street in the opposite direction of the Enforcer's trucks.

"We'll need to shake them," I said as we ran. "We'll finish circling around, and then use the houses to lose them."

The Enforcers were between us and my territory. We were one turn from going in the right direction, but it would require crossing Amica's street and exposing ourselves. I pulled her into the space between two houses and we ran back that way, slowing to a walk as we neared the street.

Our sudden exit had put some distance between us and our shocked pursuers, but not enough. I could hear them searching for us. I paused before looking out from the dubious shelter afforded by the house on our lefts' excessive, half-dead landscaping, watching the street ahead. The Enforcers were driving up the street. They would be passing by... now.

One, and then both, Enforcer vehicles passed in front of us, turning to go toward the street we had just run down. As soon as they were past, I tugged on Amica's sleeve and we started off again. Shouts followed us as a few Enforcers who had been watching Amica's house go up in flames saw us and tried to call back their fellows who had just driven in the opposite direction.

We ran flat-out for several minutes, as long as we could before Amica had to stop to catch her breath. I had confused our trail as well as I could, shifting our direction often as we passed through the dense, confusing neighborhood.

By the time we had to stop, I was fairly sure we had shaken the Enforcers.

"We're lucky they aren't well-organized or terribly smart," I commented to Amica, who was clutching the stitch in her side. I was a little out-of-breath, but otherwise fine. I would have to eat before too long, though, to avoid an unfortunate incident later.

Amica nodded her agreement, but didn't speak.

As I waited for my human companion to catch her breath, Ash came up and sat down beside me, panting but watching attentively around us. She didn't seem particularly alarmed, which was a good sign.

Why *had* the Enforcers shown up when they did? It seemed an odd coincidence that they arrived right after Amica returned home. Had they counted on me being there, or was that merely coincidence? After the letter she had apparently gotten from the pack, it seemed just a bit too suspicious that the Enforcers happened to raid her house the same day.

It looked like she had worn out whatever tolerance there had been for her independent investigating.

"We should keep moving," I said after a couple minutes. "Are you good to run?"

She didn't look enthusiastic at the prospect of running again, but she nodded. This time, we went off at a more sustainable pace.

The day was moving into evening by the time we reached my house. I had Ash and Amica pause on the near side of the street before I crossed to my house and cased it out, making sure no-one was watching for my return.

I gestured them over and unlocked the door, locking it again behind us and closing off the dog hatch. I then went around and closed any open curtains, lighting some candles for the sake of Amica's sight.

Shadow was overjoyed to see us. He spent several minutes sniffing all three of us, whining at and catching up with Ash, and leaning against me as if he was afraid I would dematerialize if he lost contact.

I checked the wound on his leg. It looked fine, and I wrapped it in a fresh bandage. When I finished, I looked up to see Amica watching me, a thoughtful expression on her face.

"What?" I asked.

She looked away, frowning. "It's strange, seeing a Wendigo so…"

"Concerned for something other than themselves?" I supplied.

She shrugged then nodded.

"Just because I have an insatiable need to eat people doesn't mean I'm not one," I replied. "You are what you eat, after all."

She didn't seem to know how to reply to that.

Oh well. What she thought of me didn't matter. I ate humans. Most humans couldn't accept that. That was reasonable and expected.

"I suggest not leaving unless absolutely necessary," I said. "I expect the Enforcers will be patrolling my territory as well as the pack's, looking for us. I'll go on a patrol and case things out once it gets a little darker." I wasn't about to admit it, but I had developed a rather unpleasant headache from looking at bright sunlight reflecting off of snow for so long. Stretching, I grimaced at the continuing twinge of pain from my ribs.

"I'm going to nap until dark. There are some books on the shelves over there, help yourself." I pointed in the appropriate direction, at a pair of bookshelves placed against the wall. They were filled with books in various states of falling apart. Many of them had been recovered from abandoned houses, and showed signs of water damage to various degrees. I had read all of them at least once.

I left Amica with the dogs and went upstairs. I wasn't sure if she would take me up on the offer of reading material or if she would follow my example and take a nap on the downstairs couch, but I didn't really care. Resting would buffer my appetite, and after the journey back to my territory, I didn't want to risk being around her too much. My retreat upstairs put some distance between myself and Amica, and once in my room her smell and presence no longer pulled so much at my hunger. I would go hunting once it became dark, and then she would be safe from me and we could devise a plan on what to do next.

Chapter 5

After a few hours of rest, my room was comfortingly dark. Slipping from the bed, I returned downstairs, hunger gnawing at me.

Amica was asleep on the couch. I stood over her for several long moments, honestly considering the cost of appeasing my hunger. Finally, I tore myself away. She was the only link I currently had to knowing my brother's fate. I couldn't afford to kill her.

I checked Shadow's leg once more. He still wasn't putting much weight on it, but he seemed anxious to get out, so when he followed Ash and myself out the door, I didn't make him stay.

Returning an hour later, I was much more relaxed. My hunger was suppressed for the moment, and I had assured myself that Enforcers were not lurking around every dark corner near my home.

I locked the door behind me once the dogs were inside. Turning to face the living room, I noted that Amica was now awake and sitting on the couch. Judging by the book sitting next to her, she had been reading in the available candle-light.

"Everything alright out there?" she asked.

I nodded. "Yeah, it's quiet."

She looked me over, her gaze lingering on my blood-stained fingers. She frowned slightly, but didn't say anything about it. "So," she said, "what now?"

I sat in an armchair facing the couch, a small cloud of dust coming up from the fabric when I did. I didn't use that chair often. Ash and Shadow followed me over and lay beside each other next to the chair. "Honestly?" I replied, "I'm not sure. The pack's aware that we're working together, and that you hold a grudge against them. They also appear to somehow be working with the government. I don't see how the two of us will be able to take them down."

Amica scowled, picking at the end of one sleeve. "I don't like to say it," she said slowly, the words bitter, "but we may have to put that off, let them fall into a sense of complacency. I've been waiting this long for my revenge, what's a few weeks more?"

I nodded. This was the conclusion I had hoped she would come to. As our situation stood, we simply didn't have a chance of dismantling or eradicating the pack.

"Would you be willing to fulfill the other half of our deal in the meantime?" I asked her after a moment, watching her closely.

She considered that. Once she was no longer of use to me, I could simply dispose of her and not fulfill my half of the agreement. She knew that, and so did I. I had no plans to do so, of course; a deal was a deal.

Finally, she nodded. "Yes. I'll help you find out what happened to your brother. We'll need to get to my old research building, though."

"Your old building?" I echoed. "I thought it was destroyed." It just so happened that that same building had been the last clue I had to my brother's fate. A large explosion had ended its use several years ago, severing my last lead at the time.

"It was damaged, but still stands. You know where it is?"

I nodded.

"Do you have a way to get there?" she asked. "A car isn't going to get through the snow, and they won't let you on a train."

"Not on a *passenger* train," I countered. "But we should be able to get there on a freight car."

"I see. That may work, as long as we aren't caught. The yards are heavily patrolled."

Shrugging, I dismissed that. "They can't watch every inch of it, and there are plenty of blind spots. I've taken the trains several times." Of course, those had all been years ago, but how much could things have really changed since then?

"It would be good for us to get out of the city for a bit, anyway," Amica said. "We've gotten too close to something both the pack and the government don't want let out."

"I agree. It is rather fishy that you've been allowed to operate without a license in the same area where an entire pack of Wendigos has gone unchecked by the government."

Amica frowned. "And as soon as we started poking our noses a little too close to that arrangement, they reacted. Violently. What do you think the government's hiding, working with the pack like that?"

"I don't know, but it probably isn't good for the Normals." I shrugged. It didn't matter much to me what happened to the self-centered, snooty, fenced-in and secure Normals that lived in more affluent areas, but it did seem unfair for something devastating to happen to the ones who weren't that wealthy...

er, lucky. Well, something more devastating than the mere existence of both perpetual winter and human-eating monsters.

"Perhaps they're trying out another super-soldier program," I suggested. "In any case, are you up for traveling now?"

"Now?" she repeated. "I don't have any supplies. I can't just…" she faltered, grimaced, then continued, "hunt down my food like you do."

I raised a brow. "Sure you can, you just need a few extra tools, and you wouldn't be hunting the same prey as me, anyway. We," I nodded to the dogs, who wagged their tails as they recognized my attention, "can hunt you down appropriate food, if you're worried about that."

"We'll have to light a fire for that."

"You *can* eat fresh meat raw."

"I'm not going to. Especially since most wildlife gets half its food from human garbage."

"Fine. The people a few houses down were preppers. There should still be something there you can use."

"Were?" she repeated, regarding me skeptically.

"Were," I verified, ignoring the implication that I ate them. "They managed to get to one of the underground doomsday set-ups when the weather turned cold, convinced that the government was covering up a nuclear war. They left a lot of their stuff behind, and no one has moved into the house since."

"Oh. Yeah, that'll work."

I stood, gesturing for Ash and grabbing an empty backpack from a pile of three or four by the door. "You stay here. I'll go grab you some supplies, and be back in less than an hour." Shadow tried to follow, but I told him to stay. Better that at least one of the dogs stay with Amica, just in case.

The house in question was just down the street. I had been through nearly all of the abandoned properties in my territory, and I knew what was left in each one, the strategic advantages or disadvantages of their locations, and which ones ended up being bought and moved into by new families. I had a lot of free time.

There wasn't any indication of Enforcers about as I made my way down the street. The sky was clear, the temperature dropping quickly as the moon shone down on the city. More stars were visible these days than in the past, as large parts of the city had gone dark in recent years.

I made my way into the basement of the abandoned house, where the old stores of food and other supplies were located. It was too dark for even my eyes to see much unaided, but the former owners had thankfully stocked up on candles as well, and lighting a couple of them I had previously placed around the room afforded as much light as I needed.

It took a bit of rifling through the abandoned supplies to find things that were both still good and would be appropriate for eating on the move, but I ended up filling the entire backpack fairly easily and headed back.

Amica insisted on going through everything herself before deeming the supplies acceptable. She left her own backpack, filled with her papers and notes, at my house, hidden deep within the basement behind a pile of junk, where no one would likely find it. I didn't think hiding it so thoroughly was quite necessary, but she insisted and it wasn't worth arguing about it.

It was past midnight when we left. The train-yard was quite a trek to the south-east, and I wanted to get there and in place before the morning freight left. Amica, however, would move more slowly through the darkness than myself. We might be cutting it close.

Shadow and Ash followed along beside us, sometimes ranging forward then coming back, keeping an eye out for anything threatening.

Progress slowed as we continued, the cold taking its toll on Amica. Her clothes were appropriate for general chill, but not for an extended trek like this.

She didn't complain, though. She slowed, but didn't stop, and I didn't stop either. The best way to keep warm would be to keep moving, and we both knew that.

It took us nearly four hours to reach the trainyard. We had to go through another Wendigo's territory to get there, though thankfully not the pack's, and we didn't run into her on our way through.

The trainyard itself was considered neutral, as many Wendigo used the freight cars for transport. Technically, doing so was illegal, but no one bothered to enforce that particular law anymore. There were more important laws to enforce, like curfew.

There were several trains waiting in the yard, strewn across more than half a dozen different tracks running parallel or crossing over each other. Most of the cars sitting in the yard weren't going to be leaving. They were far too rusted to move cargo efficiently, and would likely remain where they were until they rusted away to nothing.

There were a few trains, though, that, while nearly as rusted as their immobile fellows, lacked that rust on their wheels, which shined dully in the starlight. One of those was our ride.

I stopped at the edge of the yard, by an empty building once used as a storehouse. The dogs stopped and sat nearby. I could see three guards, but they didn't seem particularly attentive. They were cold and sluggish, and probably wanted nothing more than to go home and sleep.

"Alright," I whispered to Amica, "stay near me when I move. It shouldn't be hard to get over to the car, but we're going to have to open the door, and that could draw attention. Hopefully it's not padlocked."

Amica nodded, her jaw clenched to prevent her teeth from chattering. I considered her for a moment, noting that she seemed on the brink of hypothermia, then turned to watch the guards for our opening.

Once I was sure we could get to the proper train without being spotted, I moved forward, trusting that the others would follow. We made it to the train without incident, and found the door thankfully unlocked.

"Keep watch," I murmured to Amica, then turned to the door. Placing my hands against the edge, I leveraged my weight against the door and slid it open.

I opened it just enough for us to slip through. Turning, I looked around again, assuring myself that the sound of the sliding door hadn't alerted anyone, then ushered everyone else in.

I entered the car last, sliding the door shut again from the inside.

It was dark in there but slightly warmer than outside, or at least, out of any breeze that exacerbated the chill.

Amica seated herself on a large box, one of several piled high in the car, their shapes barely discernable in the darkness. She curled her legs up to her body, hugging them tight with her arms, shivering heavily now that she had stopped moving.

"Keep moving your fingers and toes," I advised. "It'll warm a bit in here with all four of us, and you can curl up with the dogs to share heat."

She nodded, rubbing her hands over her legs. "Don't know how you stand it," she said.

"What?" I asked, sitting on a box across from her.

"The cold. Doesn't it bother you?"

I shrugged. "There haven't been many scientific studies published on *Wendigos*," I said. "I've thought over it myself, and I think it's most likely a combination of our metabolism and our proteins. Our metabolism runs faster than a human's, that's part of why we have to eat so often. I suspect our proteins are more tolerant of varying temperatures, and there may be some sort of anti-freeze in our bodies that keeps frostbite at bay. There are some animals that produce such chemicals."

She was quiet for a long moment. "You sound awfully knowledgeable on those sorts of things."

"I used to be a biologist."

"You... before?" Her question was uncertain, as if she were hesitant to ask.

"Yeah."

"What happened?"

I sighed. "I was a natural biologist. I studied rodents in forest ecosystems; how their numbers were affected by varying food levels once the cold hit, and how that affected the rest of the food chain. I was working on a field study during the first months of the outbreak."

"Oh." Amica was silent for a long moment, and I was uncertain if she was going to ask more of me. She seemed curious, but it must be difficult, realizing that the monster sitting across from you was once human like yourself.

"How… how did it get to you?" she finally asked.

"A newly-changed individual came through the woods. I don't know where he came from. He attacked me, but I always carried a gun, so… I killed him. However, he did get a bite on me, and since that was when whatever caused the change was still active…"

"You were infected and became a Wendigo yourself," she finished. "What was it like?"

"I don't remember much," I replied slowly. "It was… painful. Extremely so. I remember feeling like I was freezing, but I never actually did. I found out later that I had been out in the woods for days before deliriously finding my way back to somewhere inhabited. I don't remember what happened then, but I'm sure you can put together the pieces."

"Yeah. I… remember the reports that came in around that time. It wasn't pretty."

"My memories started clearing after that, though it still took a while to piece together rational thoughts. I…" I sighed. "I started to feel a lot of guilt then, over what I was, what I did."

"That is the normal reaction to doing such things."

I chuckled. "It doesn't do any good, though. I can't change myself back. I need to eat, regardless of whatever any morals say. The most I can do is make the deaths of my prey quick."

"That's noble," Amica said sardonically, "but you're still killing them."

"If I were to try not to," I replied steadily, "were I to not eat anyone, I would lose control, and then far more would die than necessary, and far more violently than when I am in control of myself."

She was silent for a long time. "Yeah, I suppose I get that. Your brother... you think I knew him?"

"Knew of him, at least," I replied, not entirely unhappy with the change in subject.

Before I could continue, the train car lurched, the two dogs scrambling to their feet unsteadily.

"It's alright," I said soothingly, my tone calming them. They lay down as the train moved forward and they realized that nothing was attacking us.

"He was involved in the Humanity project," I continued. "Given that his brother turned and he did not, he was a person of interest in the isolation of an immunity factor."

"Oh." She fell silent again. "I... wasn't directly involved with that."

"No, but you worked in the same building and were funded by the same company. You're my only lead."

"I'll do what I can," she replied, "but I can't promise I'll be able to get into the proper files."

"And I can't promise we'll actually be able to take out the pack."

"That's fair."

Chapter 6

We fell into silence, the rocking of the car soothing once the train got going. The air inside the car warmed up slightly after a while, and between that and curling up with the dogs, Amica's shivering gradually tapered off.

I could tell by the sound of her breathing that she dozed off after a while. I didn't bother waking her, she could sleep until we reached our stop. We would have to switch to a different train eventually, but that wouldn't be for several hours.

I wasn't tired, myself. Except from some continued tenderness around my ribs, my wounds had largely healed. That was a good thing, as well; if I were still devoting energy to healing, it would have been much more difficult to travel in an enclosed space with a human for several hours.

With nothing else to do, my thoughts turned toward planning. Amica's doubt over being able to actually access information on my missing brother didn't really bother me. I knew she was a long shot to begin with, but she was better than nothing and she was what I had.

My brother Ryan had gone missing nearly a year after I changed. He had enrolled in a government-sponsored study of those who had family members changed into Wendigos. At that time, the change was still contagious. Whatever caused it to go dormant had yet to happen, and there was still panic about just how the infection was spread.

Some people thought the change was caused by a virus, others by prion-like proteins. No one knew for certain. That was part of what the government studies had been for, including the project Amica had worked for.

I had tried to go back to my family soon after my change. It hadn't gone well. They considered me a stranger, the person I had been dead with the advent of the monster I had become. Never mind that my mind was still there, my personality, *me.* It stung at first, but after a very close call between myself and a cousin, I left, and did not contact them again. Ryan was the only exception, the only one who still thought I was myself.

I kept track of them, of course. My newly-acquired appetites didn't erase my other emotions, or my memories. I remembered clearly when my brother signed up for the research program, and when the family realized he wasn't coming back. They had tried to get the police to look for him, but there were too many missing-persons cases already, and they simply told my family that he had likely been turned into a Wendigo and to consider him lost.

They accepted that explanation.

I did not.

After that, I spent a few months investigating government-sponsored studies, but I didn't get very far. As a Wendigo, I wasn't allowed anywhere near government-controlled buildings. Back then, too, I lacked the self-control I now had. If I got angry, if I got frustrated, if I let my emotions slip for just a moment, the hunger would drive me to kill.

There were many who died needlessly by my hands, but, as I had told Amica, there was no point in feeling guilty about it. I did what I did, and back then, I could no more control my hunger than a fledgling bird could control its wings to fly. It took me a couple years to really come to terms with such a mindset, but the alternative was insanity by guilt.

I hadn't spoken to any of my family besides my brother since they cast me out, and after my brother disappeared and they stopped looking for him, I had gradually stopped even looking in on them. I had no idea, now, how they were doing, or how many of them were even still alive. My focus had shifted to the one whom they had counted a lost cause but who, unlike me, might not actually have been.

The train rocked on. Gradually, I too dozed off, the rhythmic movement calming.

I awoke to the sound of rustling in the dark, instantly alert. I tensed for a moment, then realized it was simply Amica digging into her backpack, and relaxed.

"You wouldn't happen to have a watch, would you?" I asked.

I heard her jump, apparently thinking she wouldn't wake me.

"No," she said, "I don't."

No way to easily tell how long we had been riding, then. Oh well, I would just have to guess.

"We should be approaching a stop soon," I said after a moment's consideration. "We'll have to get off and switch to a different train, which will take us the rest of the way."

"Do you know how long that will take?" she asked.

"A couple more hours," I replied. "We'll have some time before we have to board that second one, so as long as we avoid getting caught, we can walk around a bit. It'll give us an opportunity to stretch our legs and go to the bathroom."

"Will you..." she trailed off, not finishing the question.

"Hunt while we're stopped?" I supplied.

"Yeah."

"No, probably not. I should be fine for a little while, now that I'm mostly done healing from that beating the pack gave me. So long as we don't have to do anything too strenuous, I should be fine. Or rather, *you* should be fine around *me*."

"I see," she replied, not sounding entirely reassured. There was the rustle of some sort of package being opened, and the smell of jerky filled the car.

The dogs perked up and crowded around her.

"I hope you were planning on sharing that," I commented, amused.

"Oh!" she exclaimed, moving the meat up out of their reach. "That wasn't terribly smart. Here, you can each have one piece. The rest is mine!"

"You better eat it quickly, then," I said, as the dogs quickly devoured the pieces she gave them.

Amica sighed, then shooed the dogs as they tried again to get the jerky from her.

I chuckled, then called the dogs to order, bringing them over to me so she could eat in relative peace. I was pretty sure at least one gobbet of drool landed on my foot, the dogs intent on the smell of the jerky, but they did stay in place.

"They listen to you well," Amica commented.

"I know how to speak to them," I replied. "Once they trust you, they'll generally follow along with what you say, if you know how to get them to understand what you want."

"How did you learn that?" she asked.

"I spent some time with some wolves a few years ago. They were released from a zoo and knew about as much as I did about hunting and living on their own. We taught and learned from each other."

"That's... kinda cool."

"I suppose. It was where I developed a lot of my self-control," I replied. "I needed it for extended periods of travel between meals."

A slight shift in the movement of the train caught my attention.

"We're slowing down," I said. "Get ready to leave."

She nodded and finished her jerky, putting everything back into in her backpack and slipping it on.

As the train slowed to a crawl, then to a stop, the dogs got excited about the eminent departure as well, catching our own eagerness to get out and walk around.

"We'll have to watch for guards and for workers unloading freight," I commented. At some point, wan daylight had seeped into the freight car, and now it was almost easy to see in there. I hoped it had clouded over, as I was not looking forward to dealing with bright morning sun after spending so long in darkness.

We waited until the train came to a complete stop, then I put my weight against the door, sliding it aside just enough for us to exit. I peeked out, squinting uncomfortably at the light, and looked for any sign that we would draw attention upon exiting. Thankfully, the car was in the middle of the train, rather than at the front, and was not actually up to the yard yet. The train would undoubtedly shift forward a few times to bring each section of its cargo up for unloading, but for now, we were just outside a small city.

"Looks clear," I said, and jumped out. The dogs followed, pushing past Amica, then she herself followed out. We went straight toward a stand of some sort of coniferous tree, slipping through and underneath the branches so that we were out of sight of anyone in the nearby trainyard.

"Do what you need to do," I said. I looked up at the sky, gauging the rough time from the sun, which was now visible above the horizon. "We probably have about an hour before the next train leaves, assuming the schedules haven't changed in a few years."

I stretched as well as I could within the confined space underneath the trees. "I'm going to look around. I'll meet you back here."

This time, I left Ash with Amica, bringing Shadow with me. He was still limping a bit, though he seemed cheerful enough. I didn't intend on going far, anyway, I just wanted to stretch my legs and see what the area was like. It had been a few years since I was last through here, and I didn't even know for certain if the territory was still occupied by the same Wendigo.

I didn't come across any others of my kind on the short walk, just some humans up quite early, rushing about on errands in the morning chill. They didn't take well to my presence. Many of them, upon recognizing what I was, simply turned and ran. They were much more skittish than those within my own territory, indicating that it was probably best that I *didn't* run into whoever claimed this territory.

Amica was under the trees when I returned. Judging by the tracks in the snow, she had left at one point, but hadn't gone very far. I was glad for that. Even with Ash as backup, it would not do for her to run into the holder of this territory without me.

"Set to go?" I asked her as I returned.

She nodded.

"Good. We have about thirty minutes until the train leaves. We should be on it as soon as possible. We'll need to get closer to the yard, though, so I can see the guards' locations."

She shouldered her backpack and nodded again. Thankfully, the weather was warming just a bit, and she didn't seem as deathly cold as she had during our first trek. Unfortunately, the cause of that increased warmth, the sun, made us all too visible. It would be a bit trickier to board now than it had been earlier.

I started out of the trees, Amica and the dogs following close behind. Our progress was slow as we tried to be sure we wouldn't be seen following the tracks into the trainyard. Thankfully, the guards were more worried about people coming from within the city than without, and we found cover behind some of the older, defunct cars.

Scanning around, I searched for the train I wanted. There were subtle differences to the engines, I had learned, that brought freight from one place to another. Generally they went back and forth to and from the same places, unless for some reason they broke down and needed to be replaced. If that had happened in the past couple years, knowing which one to take would simply be a guessing game.

We were lucky, though. The engine I was searching for was indeed still in service. "That's the one we want," I said quietly, pointing it out. "We'll hop on a car as soon as no one's looking."

It took a few minutes to be sure of our opening. This trainyard was better-guarded than the one back home, and it was becoming increasingly busy with workers coming in to load and unload freight. We would have to move soon, or miss our chance entirely.

One more glance around the trainyard, and I moved. I went quickly to a car, wasted no time in sliding it open, and ushered the others in before jumping in myself and pulling it shut.

This car smelled sweet, and when I checked one of the boxes, I found that they were filled with apples. I whistled. "These are going to cost a pretty penny when they get where they're going."

Amica came over. She looked over them for a moment, then pulled off her backpack, grabbed several, and stashed them away.

I chuckled.

"What? They aren't that common up our way, especially not going into winter."

"I know," I replied. "Apples are one of the hardier fruits, but still, late-season apples will fetch a good price in Columbus."

She nodded. "I don't think they'll miss half a dozen."

"Probably not."

She grabbed one more and bit into it as she sat on another box. I closed the one I had opened and sat as well, watching her.

"Are you going to eat any?" she asked.

"I don't have an appetite for those sorts of things," I replied.

"Oh." She frowned, looking down at her apple. "Is it... an "I don't want to eat this" sort of thing, or an "I can't eat this" sort of thing?"

"More of a can't. I can get away with… non-human meat, but it doesn't quiet the hunger as well, and anything else just doesn't agree with me. It doesn't make much sense, since human meat really isn't that different from any other, but…" I shrugged. "Maybe there's something specific that humans have that other animals don't."

"Ahh." She eyed her apple, but now looked as if she had somewhat lost her appetite. "What about water?"

"Oh, we drink the same as anyone else. Well, drink water. It's quite difficult to get drunk; my metabolism processes alcohol too quickly, which incidentally makes me hungrier. Not a good idea, generally. As a bonus, though, our core temperatures run a little too warm for any human pathogens to survive, so we don't get sick, though there may also be some other factor that makes us distasteful to human microbes. It's kind of nice, never having to worry about getting a cold."

"That does sound nice," Amica replied, and apparently decided that she did have appetite for her apple after all. It would be a shame to let it go to waste.

We lapsed into silence, the car lurching as the train finally started to move and gradually sped up, the car settling into the familiar rocking motion.

"How do you know this way so well," Amica finally asked after several minutes.

"I traveled it frequently the first couple years, while I was actively looking for Ryan. My family lived in Columbus, and that's where the study he volunteered for was, but by the time he disappeared, I had already left the city and established my own territory in Chicago. I would come back every so often to check on my family, and more often once Ryan was reported missing. What about you? You did research in Columbus, what made you move?”

“The research fell through,” she replied. “What I was studying… wasn’t viable. So, I took my daughter and we moved out to somewhere where there were, supposedly, fewer Wendigos.” She laughed ruefully. “Look where that got us.”

“There are fewer as you go West,” I agreed. “But only in rural areas. The country is isolated enough that many places wouldn’t have been hit by the initial infection. Not enough to eat, either.”

“Isolation doesn’t do you much good when you can’t grow anything,” she commented.

“True. A lot of people moved into the cities as the cold weather patterns became entrenched, which has just made the country more isolated.”

She was quiet for a moment, thoughtful. “You ever think of moving out there?” she asked. “Just coming in for… supplies?”

I shook my head. “I’d go crazy, literally. One bad snowstorm where I couldn’t get to somewhere populated, and I would get hungry enough to lose any sense of self I have. In the city, even in the worst weather, there’s always someone stuck out in the snow. Someone with no home, or whose family turned them out. I don’t go hungry, and they aren’t left to suffer a lingering death by hypothermia or pneumonia.”

“Your view on life is dark, you know that?”

“I don’t see how it can be anything but. I may be a monster, but at least I don’t beat people near to death just for being caught outside their houses after dark, and then leave them to freeze.”

Amica shuddered. "Those Enforcers are as bad as Wendigos," she said. "No offense."

"None taken. Most Wendigos really aren't quick with their hunts. Some like to play with their food, like cats. I," I reached out and ruffled Ash's fur, "prefer dogs."

"You are more... rational than most Wendigos," she said, speaking deliberately and watching me closely, as if worried something she said would be offensive. "More controlled. Is that because of the dogs?"

"Sort of," I replied, not at all offended by her question. "Having some creature to relate to, to look after, certainly helps. I think... some of it came from looking for my brother. The search for him, after my family wrote him off as a lost cause, occupied enough of my mind that my hunger sometimes... took a back seat."

I had lost control of myself several times during my search for any possible clues or leads, actually, having pushed myself a bit too long before realizing just how hungry I was. I knew better now, and always tried to eat before I reached that point.

Again, we lapsed into general silence. The dogs dozed, and so did Amica. My own thoughts, however, were wandering too much to allow that. Old memories I hadn't thought about in years were resurfacing, and I wasn't entirely sure that was a good thing.

A Wendigo can't afford to be sentimental. Sentimentality led to guilt, which led to repression, which led to an explosive loss of control, which led to targeted repercussions from the Normals and to death. Most Wendigos had not lived long past the initial change. Those that remained were the strong, the smart, the clever, the controlled. The survivors.

I thought back to when I established my own territory. There had been a pair of Wendigos claiming the area then, a couple who had apparently changed together. They had held a piece of territory twice as large as the one I currently held, and were, unquestionably, ruthless. They hunted who they pleased, where they pleased, with no regard for keeping out of the spotlight of government Enforcers.

They hadn't lasted more than a few months.

I was living in the shadows at that time, having come back to the city, drawn in by easier prey. There are sometimes one or two weaker Wendigos lurking within the territories of stronger ones. So long as they aren't caught, they can eke out an existence, and if something happens to the owners of that territory, they can try and make a quick move to take over. I smiled to myself at the thought. There had been one other trying to contend for what was now my territory, a vicious individual who rather liked physically tearing his victims apart. It had been a tough fight, but I had ultimately driven him out.

With that thought, my smile waned and I looked over at Amica. I wondered if he had ended up over with the pack, as one of those who killed her daughter.

Chapter 7

The sudden stopping of the train woke us all. The wheels screeched as the whole train lurched to as quick of a stop as a thing that large and heavy could come to.

The dogs scrambled to their feet, and I wasn't far behind them.

"What's happening?" Amica asked, climbing to her feet after us.

"I don't know, but probably nothing good," I replied. "Get ready to move."

She nodded and slung her pack over her shoulders.

I listened closely at the door, trying to figure out what may be happening outside, but wasn't able to hear anything.

Very carefully, I cracked open the door, looked, and didn't see anything either. I opened it a bit more, enough to stick my head through and look toward the engine at the front of the train. We were far enough back that it was difficult to see details, but it looked like there was something large blocking the track ahead of the engine. A fallen tree? I wasn't sure. Whatever it was, it wasn't good. The train systems were the most efficient means of transporting goods these days, and the tracks were kept well-cleared. If one was blocked...

"We should go," I said quietly, pulling my head in.

"What's wrong?"

"Possibly a hold-up. Come on." I shoved the door open a bit more and slipped out, turning to help Amica down into the knee-high snow.

The dogs followed, and together we headed toward the nearest tree-line. As we did, I spared a few glances toward the engine. I could spot movement up there now, more than was warranted from just a conductor and a few assistants. Maybe they brought some guards with them? If my suspicion was right, they would need them.

As we made it to the tree-line, a loud call sounded from the direction of the engine, followed by several other voices joining in with a raucous, off-key howling.

"What is that?" Amica whispered.

"People," I replied. "Raiders. They block the tracks then plunder trains for food and other supplies."

She raised both brows skeptically. "And they get away with it?"

"Sometimes. The best groups are efficient. If the conductor got a call in to the Enforcers, it'll be no less than ten minutes before backup gets here by snowmobile. In that time, they'll have packed up as much as they can carry, stashed a few more loads in the woods to come back to later, and disappeared."

"Won't their tracks be followed?"

"Depends on how good they are at obscuring the trail. Come on, we should get away from here; most independent tribes aren't friendly, and they'll outnumber us."

She nodded. I turned and headed deeper into the trees. It wasn't a very large strip of forest, a remnant of a windbreak once placed between a farm field and the train tracks. Now, when we broke out of the trees, we came out into a snowy field populated by shrubs and bushes, with the tips of tall, dead grasses poking up out of the deep snow.

"We should stay close to the tree-line," I said, "and head away from the engine. Once we're sure they're gone, we can go back and follow the tracks. They'll lead us to a town eventually."

"Do you know how far away from Columbus we are?" Amica asked.

I shrugged. "Probably no more than an hour or two by train. The priority now is staying out of the way and…"

The sound of breaking branches and crunching snow stopped me, the sound quickly followed by a pained yelp. I turned back toward the sound, searching for its source. There, several yards away in the tree line, was a young man. He was at the base of a heavily-branching tree, likely his former hiding place until he had spotted us and jumped down to either engage or report.

Something wasn't right, though. He wasn't moving from where he sat in the snow, staring at us wide-eyed. I stalked closer, the others close behind me. As I approached, the smell of blood reached me, and I stopped. My attention riveted on him, no longer simply attentive but now with the sudden roaring of my hunger pressing my entire focus on killing and devouring this wounded prey.

The young man paled further as he recognized what I was. There was a jagged piece of wood sticking out of his calf, torn all the way through his snow-pants. Likely it had been a sapling he had jumped down on. The fabric around the tear was quickly becoming wet with dark, warm blood.

"No, no, no," he mumbled nervously, obviously aware of his situation. He tried briefly to move away from me, his movements aborted with a cry of pain as he shifted the wood sticking through his leg.

I took a step forward, then another. I was hungry, and he was helpless. It was just the order of things… I stopped at the sound of a gun's hammer being pulled back behind me.

"Jason!" Amica snapped.

I growled, not turning away from the wounded young man on the ground. There was some reason why eating him would be a bad idea, but I couldn't bring myself to think too much about that at the moment.

"Jason, you're going to get us killed. Back away."

She spoke sense. If I attacked him, he would scream. If he screamed, his comrades would be on us in an instant. Although, a quick enough strike to the neck would be an instant death. No one would hear.

No, no, I had to think past my hunger. It was surprising that other raiders weren't already showing up. If he had been up in the trees playing lookout, surely there were others…

I forced my gaze away from the young man, scanning the trees around us. Now that I was looking, I spotted at least half a dozen, far enough away to avoid my own reach, but each with a bow trained on me or my dogs.

I closed my eyes and stepped back, the effort of will immense. I didn't want to step away from such an easy kill, from all that helpless flesh…

Punching a tree isn't good for your hand, but the pain certainly brings you back into focus. My bloodied knuckles and possibly-dislocated finger were enough to bring me back to my senses. Amica lowered her gun, and before me, the young man fell back in a relieved faint.

As I stepped back to join Amica, the raiders climbed or jumped down from the trees and stepped forward, four of them going to the wounded lookout. The other two came toward us, arrows nocked, though they paused at the loud growling and raised hackles of my dogs. I placed a hand on each of them and they calmed a bit, though they remained tense.

The two raiders covering us were joined by three more a minute later, each new-comer shouldering a bulging-full pack.

No one spoke. They regarded us for a moment, and we regarded them. The young man, apparently awake again, made muffled groans as he was moved, and my attention shifted to him again. His appearance had brought up my hunger as a raging, gnawing urge, but I suppressed it in favor of survival, which was a pressing-enough excuse for now.

I looked back to the raiders facing us. They didn't look like they were going to outright kill us, but I was sure they weren't just going to let us walk away, either. They pointed after a line of others, who were walking off along the tree-line, apparently wanting us to follow them.

We followed them. It was that or be shot, and I didn't much want to be shot.

"Follow their footsteps exactly," I advised Amica quietly. "It hides sign of how many people actually went this way."

From behind me, I heard a surprised grunt. "You're familiar with us, Wendigo?"

"A bit," I said, glancing over my shoulder.

A middle-aged woman followed behind us, her face rough and creased by wind and cold. A hood covered most of her hair, though from what I could see it appeared to be blonde. She had

78

a bulging-full pack of her own, and was carrying a machete in one hand. Undoubtedly she would use it if we proved to be trouble.

"I came into contact with several independent settlements back before I settled down in the city," I continued.

She raised a brow. "I'm sure you did. Not much to eat out in the wilds, is there."

"Nope."

Amica looked back at me, frowning.

"What?" I asked, giving her a small smile. "I do what I need to do to live, and so do they. I didn't kill their wounded lookout, so they didn't kill us as soon as they caught us. Most Independents have a strong sense of justice. An eye-for-an-eye sort of thing."

I looked back at the woman behind us, who looked faintly amused. "Isn't that right?" I asked.

"That doesn't mean we won't kill you when we get back," she said, "or if you cause us any problems on the way there."

I shrugged. "We're alive for now."

The dogs seemed to catch on to the walking in line thing, and walked in front of us, also in line. To the front and back of our little group were more raiders, all moving in line.

They blended in well with the tree-line, their clothes all shades of gray and brown to camouflage with the snowy landscape. I, too, blended in fairly well, with my own gray outfit, though I lacked the rough patterning to break up my outline. Amica stood out a little more, though, in a dark blue coat.

Noting movement from the corner of my eye, I looked over, then tapped Amica on the shoulder, pointing toward the source. "See the raiders over there?" There were three raiders walking in a careful line, away from the main group. "They're laying a false trail. There should be a few other groups doing the same thing. The trails will cross each other several times, muddying the trail. There's likely someone at the back of this group obscuring this trail at the same time."

She watched the others laying the false trail for a moment, then turned back to face ahead and continued on.

We lapsed into silence as we continued walking. The area used to be quite heavily farmed, with fields separated by lines of windbreaks and occasional larger pockets of forest. There were a few roads as well, some of them cleared but more of them covered in at least a few inches of snow. None of them looked like they were used very often.

After nearly half an hour, we turned down a cleared road, our footprints much less evident on the hard surface. The wind was picking up as well, which helped to further clear signs of our passage.

We turned off again a few minutes later, entering a forest. This forest was older than the others, the trees larger. It had likely been a state park or a nature preserve of some sort. A good place to hide from the authorities.

After walking for fifteen or so minutes more, during which time I noticed Amica starting to shiver, we started to see signs of habitation. There were ropes and platforms in the trees, with lookouts on many of the platforms. They watched as we entered, bows in their hands. Guns would have been more efficient, but louder, and they didn't want to risk bringing attention to themselves. A good shot with a bow could kill someone just as dead.

As we went deeper, we started seeing structures on the ground. They were mostly wooden, low-set huts, concealed by brush and snow. There weren't any fires, as smoke during the day would draw attention. Fires would be lit inside the buildings in the evening, as the sky became dark enough to hide the smoke.

We walked through the settlement, people coming out to watch as we passed, initially in celebration of the returning raiders, then in consternation at the sight of us two outsiders.

The line started dispersing as we reached what was probably the center of the settlement, the haul from the train being taken to several different storage locations.

I didn't see where they had taken the injured look-out, but it was probably straight to whatever played the role of a medical facility here. We stopped walking as the line dispersed, the two dogs coming to sit beside me and Amica placing one hand on her holstered gun. The raider who had been walking behind us remained, passing her pack to someone else to take care of.

Glancing up at the trees, I could see several people who had their bows trained on us, ready to shoot should we prove dangerous. Well, actively dangerous. I was dangerous as a general rule, but I wasn't actively killing anyone right now.

The tableau remained for several moments, then someone emerged from one of the huts before us. He was tall, and nearly as gaunt as myself. I almost thought he was a Wendigo at first, but his skin was too flushed, his proportions fully human without the too-long arms and fingers that characterized a Wendigo. No, he was just very skinny.

He was dressed in similar garb to the rest of the Raiders, winter-camouflage-patterned coat and snow-pants and good waterproof boots, but he also sported a cloak made of what looked to be a bear pelt.

Show off.

"Who are they?" he asked, addressing the raider who had walked behind us. She stepped forward.

"They were on the train," she said. "This one," she pointed at me, "refrained from eating a wounded look-out, so we didn't kill him."

I smiled, baring my teeth at him just a bit.

The man raised a brow. "Really? A Wendigo not eating helpless, bleeding prey? For the sake of what?"

"His own life, presumably," the woman replied dryly. "He is familiar with our manner of settlement."

Beside me, Amica shifted. I wasn't sure whether she was trying to warm up or was bothered by the continued discussion that completely excluded us.

The man glanced at her, then at me, then at the dogs.

"They have dogs," he commented.

"I believe they're the Wendigo's," the woman replied. "They seem well-behaved, though protective."

The dogs were sitting next to me, one on either side. They were calm enough, but they sat alertly, taking in the smells and sounds of the new place.

"So," the man said, stepping forward a few more steps to stand directly in front of me, "what's your story, Wendigo?"

"We were travelling to Columbus," I replied coolly, watching him closely but non-aggressively. "Your people held up our means of transportation."

"A Wendigo travelling with a human?" he asked.

82

"I am standing right here," Amica snapped.

He turned slightly to look at her, brow raised.

"Yes, we're travelling together," she said. "Or were, until you lot messed it up."

He nodded, then looked back at me. "Do you have a name?"

"Yes."

He watched me, apparently waiting for a further answer.

"I am Jason," I continued, after letting the silence drag on just enough for discomfort. "This is Amica. We made a deal of mutual benefit, and are currently working together."

The man nodded. "I am Allen, currently the leader of this group." He stepped past us, looking around at the settlement. "We've been here for nearly a year. If you compromise the safety of the settlement in any way, you will be executed. Both of you. And your dogs."

Beside me, Amica seemed more than a little peeved.

I nudged her.

"He's ignoring you on purpose because I'm perceived to be the bigger threat," I whispered to her. "Keep it that way."

She scowled but remained silent.

"If we're such a potential threat," I continued, louder, "why did you bring us back?"

"That is a very good question," Allen replied, looking at the woman who had followed us on the march back to the settlement. "Lena?"

The woman shrugged. "Andrew jumped out of his tree right in front of the Wendigo. He landed on a sapling and impaled his leg. The Wendigo didn't attack. So, in return, we brought them back."

"Yes, yes, we've gone over that," Allen said, waving away the explanation. "But you could have simply dropped them off at a road on the way here. Why bring them all the way?"

"I thought they could be valuable," Lena replied, glaring in defiance and daring him to deny the claim. "A Wendigo with this level of self-control could be invaluable."

"He still needs to eat," Allen replied, "regardless of how much self-control he has. Are you willing to endanger members of the settlement for a chance at a more successful raid?"

Lena scowled, but she shook her head.

"We're not going to stay," I stated. "We have business elsewhere."

"We're not going to keep you here," Allen replied after a moment's consideration. "But it may be better to wait until dark before leaving."

I glanced up at the sky. It would be several hours until dark. The darkness would afford us cover as we left and, eventually, approached the city, but it would also be colder, and I wasn't sure how far we would have to go.

"How far away is the city?" I asked.

"Several miles," Allen replied. "You'll have to get back to the tracks and either follow them or catch another train. I suggest the latter."

"The next one comes after dark?"

He nodded. "Near ten o' clock."

I looked over to Amica. "Up for hopping on another train?"

"I'll manage," she replied. "As long as I can warm up first. I don't know if I can get back like this."

I nodded. "We'll leave after dark."

Allen gestured to a few other humans standing to the side. "Take Amica to the guest shelter; make sure she's properly fed. Lena," he looked to the woman.

Lena straightened. "Sir?"

"You're tasked with watching the Wendigo. Gather a few others if you want. See he's comfortable, but brook no uncontrolled behavior."

She nodded.

"You'll be alright?" Amica asked me.

"Ehh, I've survived worse than paranoid Normals," I replied. "I'll be fine. Go warm up, we'll need to move quickly tonight."

She nodded and turned, heading off with a couple of the raiders. I remained there with Lena and Allen. After a moment, Allen, too, turned, going back to his shelter.

"Do the dogs follow you everywhere?" Lena asked.

"Not if I tell them they should stay," I replied, "though they may wander a bit if on their own."

"Are they aggressive?"

I looked down at the dogs, raising a brow at her question. Ash and Shadow were sitting quietly but attentively beside me. "Not without reason."

She nodded. "Alright, bring them with. I'll take you to my shelter. You'll want to dry off, if nothing else."

It was true that my pants had gotten rather wet with the trek through the snow. I didn't mind the cold, but cold and wet could get uncomfortable.

"Lead on," I said, and whistled for the dogs to follow.

Chapter 8

We walked for a few minutes, following a well-worn path through the snow and passing several low-built shelters. They didn't look very spacious, the ceilings very low, but I knew from past experience that their appearance belied their actual size.

Finally, Lena stopped outside one of the shelters, glancing back at me to make sure I was still following. She didn't seem terribly worried that she was going into a shelter alone with a Wendigo. She was either brave or foolish, or perhaps she was simply self-assured that she could take me out before I could take her down.

She went inside, ducking through the thick blanket hanging over the short door. I followed, the dogs behind me. I had to duck down much further than she did, but once inside, the floor sloped quickly downward into an almost cave-like room dug into the earth. The roof of the shelter arced overhead, but at least half of the shelter itself was located underground. It helped to moderate the temperature, keeping it warm for several hours after the night-time fires had to be extinguished. At the top of the shelter, at the apex of the roof, a thick wooden shutter-like flap was currently closed. At night, it would be opened to release smoke.

Even with no fire, the shelter smelled strongly of woodsmoke. Behind me, one of the dogs sneezed a few times at the sudden strength of the smell.

"This is it," Lena said, gesturing around the single room. To the right, a series of shelves had been carved into the earthen wall, and were stacked with dried food, clothes, and several random-seeming knick-knacks. A bed stretched across the far wall, and a simple desk and chair were to the left.

"Not bad," I said. "Not quite as deep as the ones at the last settlement I visited."

"Have you visited many?" she asked.

"Only a few," I replied, seating myself against the rounded wall. Ash and Shadow came over and sat beside, and nearly on top of, me. "I spent a few months in one, until they were routed by some government Enforcers."

Lena scowled. "Fucking vultures," she said. "Most of them just like to feel important, with no cares about the consequences."

"There aren't any consequences," I pointed out, "for them. They do their job and they're safe. Why care about anyone else?"

She nodded emphatically. "Hey, are you hungry?" She paused as she realized what she said, turning white. "Wait, sorry, bad question."

I shrugged. "It is rather pressing, after that lookout fell in front of me, but manageable for now." Barely. I hoped the last leg of the train ride to Columbus wouldn't be long, because between the hike back and the time spent riding, I would be on the edge of control by the time we arrived. So long as nothing unexpected happened, Amica should be fine. Probably.

Lena regarded me thoughtfully for a long moment, then nodded. "Alright. I can't exactly offer you your... preferred food, but I could get you something else, if that would help."

Other meat *could* take the edge off my hunger, enough at least to lower the danger of me eating someone next to me.

"That would be great," I replied.

She nodded. "The hunters came back with a deer a few days ago. I think there's still a bit stored. Stay here and I'll go get it."

I remained where I was while she went to retrieve the venison. I wasn't tired, not after napping so much on the train, so there was little danger of me dozing off again. It was an odd situation we found ourselves in. Lena seemed oddly trusting, and adamant about my potential usefulness. I wasn't sure where she got that mindset, but it wasn't a very good one in my opinion. As a general rule, relaxing around Wendigos wasn't smart for Normals, even around more rational ones. And welcoming a Wendigo into a human settlement? Well... I knew first hand it wasn't unheard of, and it had worked, for a time. That didn't mean it would work again. Allen didn't seem like someone who would be comfortable with the measures necessary to allow my happy existence within the settlement.

Lena was correct, though, in the idea that I could be useful. Having a Wendigo with them on raids would significantly lower the threat posed by Enforcers, and it would also help defend the settlement itself against Enforcer attack, providing precious time for a get-away. Of course, the high risk of that set-up wasn't really so great for the Wendigo in question, unless proper compensation was provided.

Again, Allen didn't seem to be the type to be comfortable with that.

I looked up as Lena returned, carrying a cloth-wrapped package.

"It's frozen," she said, "but at least some of it should thaw before you have to leave."

I shrugged. "It'll be fine. You brought quite a bit."

"I figured the dogs would want some too."

"Thoughtful of you."

She set the package down on the desk, unwrapping the blanket from around it to show me. Inside were several chunks of meat, varying in size from quite small to rather substantial. The dogs caught the scent immediately, frozen though it was, and perked up, sniffing the air. She left it there to let it thaw.

"In fact," I continued, "you're very thoughtful toward someone you really should have left back at the train, or on the road halfway here. Why are you so comfortable around me?"

She sat against the leg of her bed, facing me. "My husband was changed into a Wendigo," she said. "He disappeared for two months just after the outbreak; I figured he was dead. When he came back he was... ragged, at best. His clothes were in tatters, his hair was tangled, he was covered in dirt and blood. But he came back, and he didn't eat me, despite all the media warnings being spread at the time."

She tilted her head back. I let her talk without interruption. "I could see it in his eyes sometimes, how hungry he was, how desperate he was. He would leave for days and come back calmer but nearly as dirty as he had been when he first returned. I would clean him up, and we would continue life. The Enforcers increased their power over the next few months, and nearly a year after he returned, they caught wind of our arrangement. They didn't like it, and they hunted him down and killed him. When he didn't come back, I went out to look for him. I never found him, but some neighborhood kids told me what happened. He had never hunted in the neighborhood. They weren't afraid of him, but..."

She sighed. "Another Wendigo claimed the territory two weeks later, and the kids sure learned fear then."

Lena tilted her head back down, looking me over. "I know most Wendigos don't have much control of themselves, but not all of them are monsters."

I laughed. She seemed surprised by the response, but didn't say anything. "You," I said through my laughter, "think I'm not a monster? You think I just do what I do in order to survive? That I don't enjoy it, I don't revel in it?" I shook my head, laughter dying away. For some reason, I felt like I had to instill some sort of caution, some sort of distance. "Do you think I don't enjoy killing? Eating? Sating that gnawing, raving hunger constantly eating away at me? I do, I won't deny it. I don't kill out of hand, and my sense of self-preservation is usually stronger than my urge to eat, but that doesn't mean I'm not a monster."

She regarded me levelly, waiting for me to finish. "No, I don't believe you're a monster," she stated. "There are plenty of human monsters, and plenty of Wendigo monsters, but you are neither."

I shrugged. "Suit yourself, but if you'll take a bit of advice? Monster or not, don't relax your attention around any Wendigo."

She sighed and stood. "I'll keep that in mind. "I'm going to go check on your friend. I'll be back in a bit."

I waited until she left before standing and moving over to the still-frozen chunks of raw deer meat. It certainly wouldn't be satisfying, but it would help push down my hunger for now, and the dogs would certainly appreciate it. I tossed a large chunk to each of them, and they set about gnawing on the frozen meat. Prying off a smaller piece for myself, I returned to my spot sitting against the wall.

Lena really did seem convinced of her belief that I, and perhaps others like me, weren't monsters. It was a dangerous position to take. I certainly wouldn't kill her unless beyond my own limits of control, but that didn't make me safe to be around. And there were plenty of other Wendigos with high levels of control who wouldn't think twice about killing a Normal just for the fun of it. Rachel, for example.

That posed another problem. What to do about that pack? I couldn't take all of them out on my own, and while Amica was a good shot with a gun, she wouldn't be able to take out more than one or two herself before being overwhelmed. Perhaps we could recruit help here; Lena at least might be interested in such an endeavor.

But that would mean bringing her, and anyone else interested, with us to Columbus first, and I didn't know what sort of environment waited for us there. The general Enforcer presence would be there, of course, but each city was configured differently, and it was long enough since I had last been there that a lot could have changed.

No, it would be too risky to bring anyone else.

Perhaps we could find back-up while in the city? Or perhaps we would find something else that could give us a leg up over the pack. I couldn't rely on such a long-shot hope, though.

I munched my way through the chunk of frozen meat, considering the range of problems before me. I was close to finding out what had happened to my brother. So close that waiting for darkness before moving on was quickly becoming frustrating. I wanted to be moving, to continue on and find out what I could.

Of course, after that I had to help Amica get revenge for her dead daughter, and *that* endeavor would likely get us killed.

But, if I knew what had happened to my brother… such a suicide mission didn't seem quite so unthinkable.

I remained immersed in my thoughts for at least an hour with no sign of Lena's return. I wasn't sure what she was doing, but whatever it was, it wasn't my business. I didn't mind her presence, but her easy-going manner around me was a bit… unnerving. I honestly didn't know how to handle it. At least Amica made no illusion against being willing to shoot me if I turned on her.

A scuffling outside caught my attention, and I looked up at the door. No one walked in, though, so I turned back to my thoughts. A few minutes later, I again heard noise of someone running by. This time it was accompanied by shouting and the sound of gunfire. As I listened, I caught the thumping of several marching feet. I frowned. That wasn't normal. Whistling at the dogs to follow, I stood and ducked out through the opening, looking around.

The settlement was in chaos. A distant rumble of engines suggested the approach of some sort of large machinery, perhaps a helicopter or large truck of some sort. The latter would have trouble getting all the way here through the forest, but it didn't look like that would be much of a deciding factor in the battle I saw before me, anyway.

What looked like dozens of men and women with government uniforms had marched on the settlement, and were opening fire to the lookouts located in the trees above.

The Independents were quickly rallying, but it was clear that they were severely outgunned. They had some guns, but they simply weren't up to par with the Enforcers', and the bows and arrows certainly didn't stack up. The Independents *did* outnumber the Enforcers, but not by much, and their numbers were quickly dropping.

The smell of blood and gunpowder flooded my nose, and the sight of people running back and forth through the trees distracted me. My attention was brought back to the moment by Ash's whining. Right. Gun-shy.

I reassured her with a quick scratch of an ear, then began ducking my way toward the direction Amica had been taken earlier. I needed her, and her dying here would do me absolutely no good.

Of course, I thought as a bullet whistled over my head, if I died here that wouldn't do me any good, either.

"Jason!"

I looked over at the sound of my name. Amica and Lena were crouching in the lee of one of the shelters, trying to avoid the gunfire. Judging by their location, they had been heading back toward me.

I glanced around, determined that the coast was clear, and dashed over. There wasn't much space for the three of us and the two dogs, and I knew we couldn't stay there long.

"We need to get out of the settlement," I said.

Lena looked like she was about to argue. I cut her off before she could begin. "We're outgunned and, by now, outnumbered. They're bringing in something big, I can hear it. We need to get going. There's nothing we can do for the settlement."

"There are children here!" Lena exclaimed.

"I am not traveling with children," I replied flatly, "and there is nothing we can do for them if we're dead. We just have to hope the Enforcers don't kill them outright. Come on, we need to get moving."

A volley of gunfire went off nearby, accompanied by a scream and a thud as a body fell from a tree onto the snowy ground. I glanced around again, seeking cover to move toward, then nodded in that direction and headed off without further statement. The others would follow, or they wouldn't. Amica would likely follow. Lena... well, if she didn't, it would be easier to travel with two people than three.

They both followed. The dogs were close on my heels as we ducked behind another hut, the humans not far behind.

We continued like that for a few minutes that seemed to stretch on forever. Run, crouch, pause, look, run again. People ran by, both Independents and Enforcers, but most of them were already intent on fighting each other and could spare no attention for us. There were a few Enforcers who came at us, but the shock of seeing both a Wendigo and two large, angry dogs bought us enough time to take them out without being shot.

Finally, we came to the edge of the settlement. The forest underbrush grew more thickly here, with occasional tangles of brambles making passage all but impossible. It would be hard going, but we needed to put as much distance as possible between ourselves and the settlement. A sound ahead caught my attention, and I gestured for Amica and Lena to wait in the dubious shelter of a cluster of brambles as I went forward to check it out. It was the wounded lookout, Andrew. I wasn't sure how he had made it all the way out here, but however he had, he had over-exerted himself in doing so. His injured leg was bleeding through the bandage, and he didn't look like he could walk much further on his own.

Again, we were caught in a tableau of mutual regard, him with fear and myself with hunger. Snarling with frustration at the war between hunger and survival in my head, I turned back, returning to the others.

"It's Andrew," I said quietly. "Come on."

"We need to take him with us," Lena stated. "I'm not leaving him here to freeze or be hunted down by Enforcers."

I started to argue, but this time Amica cut in. "We can't save everyone, but if we can save *someone* it's worth it. Show us where he is."

I grimaced but nodded, turning and heading back toward where the wounded lookout was.

They didn't waste time talking, thankfully. While the dogs watched our back and flanks, I took lead, with Amica and Lena supporting Andrew between them.

Out here, there was far less activity. The sounds of the battle behind us quickly faded as we pushed our way through the brambles, the sounds muffled by snow and underbrush. I was a little surprised to see that there were no Enforcers out here, hunting down stragglers, but I was sure they would come back later. We needed to get out of their expected range before they started sweeping the entire forest.

Or... they could... oh.

"Lena," I whispered, falling back a bit to walk beside her, "how many settlements have you lived in?"

"This was the third," she said. "The other two were routed, like this one."

"Any forested?"

"The first."

"How did they destroy it?"

She grew pale and stopped, bringing our little party to a standstill. "They napalmed the forest," she said.

I nodded. "That's what I thought. Come on. If we're not going to leave him," I nodded toward Andrew, "we need to at least move *faster*."

There wasn't any argument. We continued on, faster this time, pushing through branches and brambles with disregard to cuts and tears to our clothing. I was fairly sure now what it was that I had heard coming closer under the sound of gunfire. Helicopters. They were bringing helicopters in not to shoot, but to set fire to the forest.

I could hear them more clearly now, and hoped that they weren't surrounding the forest. If they started at the settlement site and worked outward, we would have a fair chance of escape. If they started from the edge of the forest and worked in... our chances of survival were lower.

"Is there a lake anywhere nearby?" I asked.

"No," Lena replied. "Well, there is, but it's in the other direction, back past the settlement."

"How close to the edge of the forest are we?"

"I'm not sure," she said, shifting Andrew's weight as he stumbled and leaned heavily on her. "In this direction... the settlement is nearly a mile in."

I frowned. Not enough time. "Faster," I said.

No one complained. They could all hear the helicopters now, and behind us the sounds of gunshots had stopped.

The Enforcers were making their escape before they could be caught in the inferno.

We pushed on more quickly still, though I could hear Andrew's breath becoming ragged behind me, distracting in its loudness. Amica and Lena, too, sounded like they were quickly tiring, having to support Andrew's weight as we moved.

The end of the forest was in sight when the helicopters flew by overhead. They began ranging along the edge of the forest a few hundred feet away, spraying a flaming, sticky chemical onto the trees, the blaze quickly spreading.

"Get into the field and cover yourselves with snow," I yelled over the noise, breaking into a full run through the last stretch of forest. I didn't want to leave the others behind, but if they couldn't make it out, staying with them wouldn't save me. "Stay under the snow until the helicopters leave."

The last few steps singed hairs from my head and scorched my coat, but I made it through. The dogs were less than a step behind me, running out ahead of me into the field. I hoped that they would simply be thought feral and ignored.

I turned back, looking for the humans. They stumbled out of the forest several seconds after me. I couldn't tell how badly they had been burned, but they were still moving, and that was what counted.

The thumping pressure of an approaching helicopter sent us diving to the ground, working to tunnel into the snow as well as we could. I hoped that everyone could get under before being seen, because a direct blast would take us all out, snow-cover or not.

We waited under the snow for what seemed an eternity, the intermittent helicopters rumbling by overhead. The heat from the fire began reaching us where we were hiding, and I hoped that our cover wouldn't completely melt before the Enforcers left.

An eternity later, the sound of the helicopters faded, leaving only the roaring of the nearby fire. Cautiously, I lifted my head, wet, thick snow falling away as I looked around. The sky was clear of machines as far as I could see.

"It's clear," I announced. "We should get moving again."

The dogs had run away from the fire. I wasn't sure where they had ended up, but they should be able to find us again. To one side of me, two forms sat up and brushed the snow off themselves, Lena and Amica. The mound that was Andrew moved a little, but didn't sit up.

I frowned, standing and walking over to him. Crouching down beside him, I brushed the snow away, grabbed an arm, and pulled him to a sitting position. He was shivering violently and looked very pale, while the snow around his leg had been dyed a bright red with blood.

My grip tightened on his arm, the smell of blood overwhelming. I had kept myself from killing this kid twice, but ... he was weak, he was nearly hypothermic, he was wounded...

"Jason?"

My name sounded like it was coming from a very long distance away. I didn't pay it any mind. I could answer *after* I sated the terrible, aching, raging hunger demanding me to tear, to kill, to eat... I grabbed his shoulder with my other hand, pulling him toward me.

"Jason!"

This time, the sound of my name was accompanied by a rock hitting my shoulder. I looked up, a snarl on my lips, to see both Amica and Lena on their feet, Amica with a handgun out and leveled at me.

98

"Jason," Amica said a third time, "stand down."

I growled at them, my fingernails digging into Andrew's arm enough to draw blood. He whimpered and tried to pull away, but was too weak to break free. I didn't want to let him go, even if part of me knew I should. The smell of blood was intoxicating, and the hunger in the center of my being demanded satiation.

I looked from the two women, to Andrew, and back again. I didn't doubt that Amica would shoot if I acted, and was it really worth dying for a meal?

Yes, I answered myself. Damnit, yes.

No, no it wasn't.

Yes, it was.

"Stand. Down." Amica repeated.

I didn't. I made a move for Andrew's throat. Amica shot.

The sudden searing pain in my shoulder brought me back to my senses. I released Andrew, stumbling to my feet and back, away from him. I could feel blood soaking into my shirt beneath my coat. My own blood, not Andrew's.

The fire still burned behind us, hot on my back. I focused on that and on the pain in my shoulder, turning away from the sight and smell of blood and the weakened, injured lookout until I could get myself under control.

Every minute we stood there in the field we were in danger of being spotted. The threat wasn't as large as it had been, with the helicopters gone, but we were still out in the open, vulnerable. We needed to get moving.

I needed to eat.

"Here."

I jumped, spinning around at a touch to my uninjured shoulder. Lena stood there, holding out a large chunk of raw venison.

"It's not what you want," she said, "but it will help."

I stared at her for a moment, honestly considering just attacking her instead, then took it. I stepped past her, past Andrew, past Amica, murmuring a half-hearted thanks that even I could barely distinguish from a growl. I continued on, across the field, walking toward the forest on the far side, sure that the others would follow me, foolish as that may be.

Chapter 9

We made camp in the forest on the far side of the field. There was some debate between Amica and Lena as to whether we should have a fire, but I didn't pay much attention. I simply sat out of the way, far enough from Andrew that I could almost ignore him.

Eventually, they decided that getting warm, especially for Andrew, who was by this time looking decidedly unwell and shivering uncontrollably, was more important than the risk that our fire would be spotted.

I rested for a few minutes before turning my attention to the burning pain in my shoulder. I ignored the others, and they let me be. It would be dangerous for them to attract too much of my attention right now, and they knew it. The bullet was still in my shoulder. I needed to remove it, so that the wound would have a chance to heal. Of course, as soon as the wound started healing, the distraction of pain would no longer be enough to keep myself from killing my human traveling companions. Not to mention that the process of healing, itself, was just going to make my hunger worse.

I grimaced as I dug my fingers into the wound in my shoulder, but didn't make a sound. It hurt like hell, but I didn't like leaving bullets in. At least I didn't have to worry about infection.

It took a minute or two, but I managed to reach the bullet. It took longer for me to get a grip on it and pull it out, growling at the pain. I didn't realize until it was out that Amica and Lena were both staring at me. "What?" I snapped.

"You alright?" Lena asked.

"No, I'm not alright," I replied sharply. "I just pulled a bullet out of my shoulder, and my every sense and thought is tuned to the fact that there is a wounded, helpless, near-dead human right over there. It is taking every ounce of self-control I have not to kill and eat every one of you. So unless you can find a fresh human corpse somewhere, I suggest not talking to me."

She stared at me.

"He's right," Amica stated. Her gun was sitting out, right beside her. The safety was off, as well, ready to immediately shoot me again if she needed to. "He's dangerous," she continued, "until he eats, and eats something other than those chunks of venison you brought with you."

Lena sighed. "Fine, sit in your corner in the dark, then."

I did.

I didn't sleep with the others. As soon as they lay down to sleep, I stood, leaving the fire and heading back across the field. At some point the dogs joined me, melting out of the darkness to brush against my legs. I was glad they had returned. It would make what I was searching for easier to find.

We reached the burned forest quickly. It was still smoldering, enough embers still glowing to faintly illuminate the immediate area.

I turned to move along the edge of the burned area, ranging along it in a steady, energy-conserving lope. Now that I didn't have to keep myself from eating someone I shouldn't, I could turn every sense to finding what I sought.

One of the dogs barked. I slowed down, continuing forward until the smell of charred human flesh reached my nostrils.

We eventually returned to the camp and after a few minutes I relaxed enough to fall asleep, the dogs curled up on either side of me.

It was well into the morning by the time I awoke. The fire had completely burned down in the night and hadn't been replenished in the daylight. The humans were all up, Lena rebandaging Andrew's wounded leg. Amica and Lena both glanced over at me as I sat up, gauging the level of threat I currently posed.

I stood, stretching my shoulder. It was painful and stiff, and my shirt was uncomfortably crusted with blood, but the wound was quite a bit better for the food and sleep.

"I'm fine," I said, in return to their continued stares. Lena continued regarding me, but Amica nodded and went back to dressing a second-degree burn on her own arm.

After a moment, Lena, too, went back to what she was doing. I walked around a bit, to the edge of the small forested area we found ourselves in, looking across to the burned remains of the large forest that had, until yesterday, held the settlement. There wasn't much to see, just blackened ground and black spikes of charred tree-trunks, standing starkly against the gray sky. I wondered if anyone else had managed to make it out. There were likely a few, but not many would have escaped both the bullets and the fire.

I returned to the campsite. Lena was just finishing up the bandaging of Andrew's leg, and had buried the old, blood-soaked cloth under the snow a short way away. I was glad for that. I was back under control, but my meal in the night had been less than completely satisfying, and I would need to eat again fairly soon.

"We should move on," I said. "The Enforcers may come back to look for survivors."

"We... should we really go with him?" Andrew asked, looking anywhere but directly at me. "What if... he..."

I sat on a nearby fallen tree, waiting for them to come to a decision. Really, I didn't care whether or not Lena and Andrew came with us. They would likely be more hindrance than help, especially Andrew, but I wasn't going to be so crass as to simply turn them away. It was up to them to decide whether or not they wanted to remain in my company.

"I'm going with him whether you two are or not," Amica said, not looking up from where she was now cleaning her gun. "We have a deal to finish."

Lena looked between Andrew, Amica, and me. Whatever she chose, Andrew would likely follow along. It wasn't like he could get far on his own with that leg, and he didn't strike me as the self-sufficient type in general.

"I think we have a better chance with them than without," Lena finally said. "There's a lot of distance between here and the nearest town, and we'll fare better as a group. If we want, we can split off there."

Andrew looked skeptical, still not looking at me, but after a moment he nodded.

"If he loses control," Amica added, "I'll just shoot him again. You'll be fine."

"I would prefer if you didn't shoot me unless necessary," I stated dryly. Being shot hurt, and the healing process only exacerbated my appetite.

"As I said," she replied, matching my gaze steadily.

I shrugged (ow). "Alright, well, since that's decided, we really should move on. Lena, where's the nearest town? The Enforcers will be watching the tracks for fleeing survivors, so that route's out of the question for now."

"Five miles to the East," she replied, putting her supplies back in her pack. Apparently she already had it ready when the settlement was attacked. Did she wear it around everywhere? I wouldn't be surprised if she did. She had survived multiple Enforcer attacks, after all. She shouldered the pack and stood.

Five miles wasn't a terrible distance, but we would have to stay off the roads, moving through the deep snow of field and forest. That wouldn't be much of a problem for me, but it would be tiring for the humans, and especially for Andrew.

Still, it was the best shot for re-stocking our supplies and gaining shelter and/or transport.

Amica, too, stood and shouldered her pack. She had bandaged one arm up to the elbow, and then again near her shoulder.

"How bad were you burned?" I asked.

"Second-degree, along my arm. None of the blisters have broken."

Andrew stood shakily. He didn't have a pack, but it would be best for him not to carry any additional weight, anyway.

"You should find a walking stick," I advised. "It'll help."

He glanced at me very briefly, then looked away and nodded.

"I'll take point," I said, now that everyone was up and ready to go. "It'll be easier for me to break a trail than for any of you. Andrew should be toward the back, so the path is already broken for him."

"I'll take up the rear itself," Lena said.

That left Amica and the dogs just behind me.

I nodded and turned, setting off toward the East. We would be walking parallel to the burned forest for a while, until we passed the extent of the conflagration, then would turn south a bit.

We had to go through a field first, moving at a snail's pace through the deep snow. The weather had warmed just enough for the snow to start melting and become dense and wet. It looked like it may snow again as well, which would be good for remaining unseen, but not good for finding our destination.

The wet snow quickly soaked through my pants and boots, and I was sure it was doing the same for the humans. The dogs, too, seemed to be having a bit of a hard time in the snow, though they followed in line as the others did.

As we reached the far end of the field, a few large, heavy snowflakes began falling around us. Once under the cover of the trees, bare through they were, the falling snow was less noticeable, but it was still evident that it was falling increasingly heavily. By the time we made it to the far side of that small forest, the visibility had decreased drastically and the wind was picking up. I looked out across the next field, not able to see much through the snowfall.

"I don't think it's safe to continue on in this," I said as the others gathered around me, also looking out into what looked like the start of a blizzard. Even among the trees the visibility had become low, as the wind whipped the snow into a wall of white.

"Agreed," Lena replied. "We should find somewhere to make camp."

"We've barely gone anywhere, though," Andrew said. "Shouldn't we try and get further away from the burned forest?"

I suspected he also wanted to get to the town as quickly as possible so that he no longer needed to be around me. I didn't blame the guy.

"We don't want to get lost in a blizzard," Lena replied. "We could veer off in any random direction and lose each other, and we wouldn't know it until the snow cleared."

"We also have wet pants," Amica interjected. "The wind will freeze them, and us."

"Campsite it is," I said, and turned to head back into the forest. There was a fallen tree not far away that had caught my eye. Its roots had torn up a chunk of earth, forming a wall-like structure with a hollow lee which was, currently, facing away from the wind.

We stumbled into the sheltered depression before spotting it, the visibility was so low. There wasn't a lot of room, but there was enough for all of us if we stayed close together. The dogs took a moment to shake the moisture from their fur once we were out of the wind, then settled in near the base of the dirt wall.

It wasn't a perfect shelter. The wind still blew in at the edges, flinging snow at us, and the temperature was steadily dropping again. It was better than being out in the blizzard, though. The humans huddled together for warmth, and the dogs and I ended up in the huddle as well, pooling everyone's body heat together. My threshold for cold tolerance was high, but freezing wet pants in increasingly low temperatures would drain my energy quickly while I compensated for the cold. It would be best not to push my limits much more around the others, especially while still healing from being shot. Didn't want poor Andrew to wind up dead, after all.

"Anyone know any campfire stories?" Amica asked after several minutes of listening to the howling of the wind around us.

"Campfire?" Andrew asked.

"You don't *need* to have a campfire to tell them," Amica replied, "but they might help occupy our attention. This storm is going to keep blowing for awhile."

"I remember we actually had one we would tell about a Wendigo at a campground," Lena said, "back when I was in Girl Scouts. That was before all this happened, though." She waved a hand vaguely around at our surroundings. "Well, the climate was changing already, but it hadn't swung around to where it is now, and actual Wendigos didn't exist yet." She glanced over at me.

"If I remember correctly," she continued, "the Wendigos in myth didn't look like the ones existing now. They were monstrous creatures with skeletal forms and antlers."

"We were named after the Native American myths," I said, "because we eat people and can withstand the cold. Since we're not dead, we weren't classified as zombies, and given our uncontrollable, ever-present hunger, Wendigo fit."

"The original Wendigo myths didn't have antlers," Andrew muttered, though he didn't seem compelled to add more.

"You do have some of the skeletal thing going on," Amica commented after it was clear Andrew wasn't saying any more. "You look emaciated."

I shrugged. "It doesn't matter how much we eat, it's all burned away too quickly to put on any weight."

"How do you handle the cold without any fat reserves?" Lena asked.

"My body burns hotter than a human's, and maybe I have a natural antifreeze of some sort in my blood that keeps it liquid. I also just... don't feel the cold."

"Does it... does it hurt?" Andrew asked.

"Does what hurt?"

"Being..." he gestured toward me but didn't finish his sentence.

"Being a Wendigo? No, it doesn't hurt. Unless someone shoots me, of course. The initial change was painful, but after that, and after I got the hunger under control, it felt good. My senses are better than a human's, and so is my physical strength. I'm faster, stronger, and can smell, see, and hear better."

"You just have to deal with the hunger," Lena commented.

"Yes. And all those other things simply make me a better predator," I said, eying her. Did she still think I wasn't dangerous, after what had happened the previous evening?

Andrew yawned. "I don't know why you let the government get away with what they do, then. If you're so strong and smart, why don't the Wendigos band together and get rid of the Enforcers?"

I raised a brow at his suggestion. "It's harder to kill us, but we can be killed. The Enforcers out-gun us just as much as they out-gunned your settlement. Moreso, in fact. And most Wendigos are barely in control of themselves even when they're well-fed. We don't work well with others. *And*, if you were to gather that many Wendigos together, what do you think would happen to the human population between them and the Capitol?"

No one spoke. What I delineated was a grim scenario, but it was precisely why there *wasn't* an army of Wendigos storming government facilities. Even packs such as the one back home were rare, and it was very good for the remaining human population that they were.

The conversation petered out after that. Between my mentioning what had happened to the settlement and the prospect of what a Wendigo army would really mean for the Normals that got in its way, everyone seemed a little... depressed. Well, what did they expect? The world was depressing.

Chapter 10

It was full dark before the storm blew itself out. We agreed to stay where we were until light, as even I found it difficult to see anything this far out in the middle of nowhere, with clouds obscuring any light that may come from the moon or stars. Remaining there for the night would also give everyone's wounds further opportunity to heal before being strained again with more walking.

The clouds had cleared by morning, the sun reflecting brightly off the freshly-fallen snow. It would be nearly blinding in the fields come midday. I wasn't looking forward to that, but it would be best to travel in the light while the others could see.

Amica and Lena were awake and up, but we let Andrew sleep as long as possible before waking him.

We headed out, continuing more slowly than the day before. It was rough going even for me. The snow was deep enough to be difficult to walk through, and it had been blown into tall drifts which required extra effort to scale. I trudged on, leaving a trail behind me for the others to follow. We crossed one field, then another, then a small forest, then another field.

We took a break around noon. The pace was still frustratingly slow, hampered by both the snow and Andrew's wounded leg. By my estimate, we had gone a little over two miles at that point, bringing us nearly halfway to the town. At this pace, it would take at least another three hours to get there. Maybe I *should* just eat Andrew.

Amica pulled some apples out of her pack and handed them around. The humans were hungry enough themselves not to be concerned by the trouble those apples had caused, and just ate them. Lena pulled out the last of her venison and gave it to the dogs. They were happy to take it, and proceeded to spend the rest of the break playing in the snow.

We didn't stay there long. We hadn't seen any Enforcers on our hike so far, but that didn't mean they weren't around, even out in the middle of nowhere. Staying in one place for too long in broad daylight was a bad idea, and would become more so the closer we got to the town.

We continued on, breaking trail through snow that occasionally neared my waist. By the time the town came into sight, even I was tiring. I was increasingly hungry, and my shoulder ached as I slogged through the deep snow. Thankfully, the others didn't try to start conversation, and the march was a silent, focused affair.

We stopped briefly when we saw the town, resting for a few minutes before continuing the last short distance. There was a short debate over whether I should accompany the others in, but it was decided that it would be better to have me and the dogs along, at least for the initial check of the town's atmosphere.

There weren't any Enforcers in sight as we approached. In fact, the town appeared abnormally empty, with very few people out and about. The roads hadn't yet been plowed from the previous day's blizzard, and it was possible they wouldn't be. Given how expensive gas was for civilians, the people here may simply have abandoned the use of motor vehicles in town.

We only saw one person out walking as we came into town, and they didn't spare us more than a glance before hurrying on their way, faster than before.

"Do you know anything about this town?" I asked Lena as we slogged through snow toward the downtown area.

She shrugged. "Not much, it was too risky to come in here often. I know there was a Wendigo that claimed it as his territory several months ago, but I would assume the Enforcers have dealt with him by now."

I grunted acknowledgement, though judging by the lack of both Enforcers and visible residents, I would guess that the local Wendigo *hadn't* been taken care of.

This meant that if I ate here, I would be trespassing on their hunting grounds. I sighed. Well, that might just have to happen anyway, and screw the consequences.

"The locals don't seem very friendly," Amica commented, watching the houses as we walked past. I followed her gaze and spotted at least three people peering through their curtains, only to, as soon as they realized we were watching, quickly pull them shut again.

"Maybe they're waiting inside for the streets to be cleared?" Amica suggested.

"The snow's just as deep in the roads as anywhere else," I said. "No one clears these streets."

It did seem odd that there wasn't any outdoor activity in this town. Many of the houses were obviously abandoned, the siding and roofing coming off and windows broken, but there were still many that looked like they could still house people.

"We should chase down the next person we see outside," I suggested. "If we can catch someone out in the open, we can hopefully get them to tell us why the town looks so... scarce."

It really didn't make sense that *none* of the roads would ever be cleared. Even if most were left to build up with snow, there should be at least one open for the import of supplies. Otherwise, this town would very quickly wither and die.

"Perhaps the main road through town will be cleared," I mused to myself.

We continued walking, heading toward the center of town. Nothing changed as we neared the downtown area. The streets and sidewalks, or at least, the areas where they should be, were still mostly empty, and the residents merely peeked out at us through their windows.

The main road was marked by a distinct dip in the level of snow, bordered by small mountain ranges of piled snow at both sides. There were several inches of snow on the road from the previous day's blizzard, not yet cleared.

"There's their supply route," I commented.

The others nodded.

"Where're the people, then?" Lena asked.

"There are businesses here," Amica commented, looking around at the buildings lining the street, "but it doesn't look like any of them are open."

"They may be waiting for the road to be cleared," I said absently, but I didn't really believe my comment. I was scanning the buildings, the alleys, anywhere where someone could hide. I spun around slowly, looking all around.

My search didn't turn up anything interesting beyond dozens of empty windows staring blankly down at us, but I had a feeling that we were being watched.

114

"We should walk down the center of the road," I said quietly, "so we're harder to ambush and don't look too suspicious."

Andrew frowned at that, but Amica and Lena responded by looking around much as I had.

"You think there's danger here?" Amica asked.

"I think we're being watched. I don't think that Wendigo's been taken care of."

We moved to the center of the road, walking through the slightly less-deep snow there.

"Do you think they'll try anything with all of us together?" Andrew asked. He was limping noticeably but had kept going this far and wasn't stopping now. I had to admit he was handling the wound well, though his gait betrayed a critical weakness that would be exploited by any half-competent predator.

I could have killed him many times over, but I needed Amica and she didn't want me to kill the clumsy former-lookout. I would prefer not to be shot again.

"Only if you lag far enough behind the rest of us," I replied, scanning the buildings to either side of us. Neither Ash nor Shadow seemed alarmed, though they were picking up on my alertness and were avidly sniffing around for anything interesting.

Ahead of us, I caught sight of someone moving down the street. I stopped, and the others stopped with me, all of us watching the figure for a long moment.

"It's a human," I said. Wendigos weren't that clumsy in snow. "We need to catch up."

"Go ahead," Amica said. "We'll follow."

I glanced back at her, raising a brow skeptically.

She had her gun out, and pointedly raised a brow back at me. Right. She could take care of a Wendigo, if they were attacked while I was up ahead. Assuming it was a single Wendigo, and assuming that Wendigo had no dogs or other backup.

Lena pulled out a large hunting knife. Well... that wasn't useless. They would be fine.

I turned and started loping through the snow, the dogs on either side of me. They quickly caught on that I was on a hunt, their tails and ears up cheerfully as they ranged beside me. I whistled them back from running ahead, not wanting to actually kill this human. I wanted answers.

As soon as she saw me, she ran. Not an unexpected reaction, but an ultimately futile one. I caught up quickly, the dogs coming around to flank her, yipping excitedly.

The woman stumbled, falling into the snow. She brought her arms up to guard her face and any attack that may be coming. For a moment, I had a severe urge to finish the hunt and go in for the kill, but information was more important.

I scowled at myself as I pushed back my hunger, and called the dogs to stand down. It took a few moments to calm them enough for them to sit, during which time the woman appeared to realize that something was not as she expected.

She lowered her arms slowly, her eyes wide as she stared at me.

The dogs having settled down, I regarded the woman, meeting her gaze. After a moment she looked away, her hands visibly shaking in fear.

"Y... you aren't... you're a..." she swallowed, "different one."

116

"Different one?" I echoed.

She flinched as I spoke.

"Not... not ours. Not our Wendigo."

"Your Wendigo? The one that claims this territory?"

She nodded, daring glances at the dogs. "Are you going to kill us?" she asked. "He... he says that if any outsiders came, they would kill all of us... not just a few like he does."

"Outsiders? Any outsiders that come here?"

She nodded again.

"Humans included?"

Another nod.

I was a little surprised by that, though it did make sense. It was a decent tactic if one's intent was to control the population and keep them from seeking outside help. It was possible this Wendigo had a few humans he kept close in his confidence, and they handled any supply deliveries that came into the town. Meanwhile, the Wendigo essentially had a cultivated herd in the rest of the town, to last as long as it took him to overwhelm their numbers with his hunger.

"We're not here to kill you," I commented, a little absently as I looked around. There was still no sign of the local Wendigo. He was watching, though, I was sure of it.

The others caught up with me and the dogs, coming to stand on either side of me.

"Hey there," Lena said, offering a hand to help the woman up. The woman looked at it like it was dangerous.

Pulling back her hand, Lena looked at me questioningly for an explanation.

I shrugged. "They've been brainwashed not to trust outsiders. She thinks we'll kill her and everyone else in the town."

"Oh."

"Did you get anything else from her?" Amica asked.

"Mostly just that," I replied. "There is a Wendigo here, claiming the territory. He's convinced the population that outsiders, Wendigo or human, will kill them all, rather than just a few at a time, as he so kindly does."

As we talked, the woman started to gather herself, positioning her feet underneath her, though she remained crouched down in the snow. She was apparently ready to try running again. It wouldn't do much good, and was unnecessary since none of us were actually going to kill her, but it was rather brave of her.

Someone spoke from one of the buildings to the left. "It is generally considered *polite* of guests to introduce themselves to the head of the household before talking to others."

Ah. There he was. This guy seemed to have a penchant for drama. It would have been smarter just to shoot us, but to each their own.

"We would have, if you had shown yourself earlier," I replied loudly, though I didn't yet look over at him.

Beside me, I could see from my peripheral vision that Amica still had her gun out, held in a steady grip but not yet up. Andrew was shifting nervously. Seriously, how had he not died years ago?

I kept my gaze on the woman crouched before us. "Go on," I said, gesturing to the right with my head for her to run off that way. "This business doesn't concern you."

She glanced over to where the other Wendigo spoke from, hesitated for a moment, then dashed off away from him and us. Ash jumped after her briefly, but I quickly called the dog back. She was hesitant for a moment to leave the fleeing woman be, but obeyed and returned.

Finally, I looked over in the direction of the voice. The Wendigo was approaching, apparently having jumped from a second-story window down to the mountain of plowed snow beside the road. He was taller than me, though not by much. His hair was military-short and black, and he sported a torn Enforcer uniform. He held himself like he was used to being in charge, used to inspiring awe. I wondered if that bravado was backed up by anything other than the terror of the residents of a small, isolated town.

"You're either brave or foolhardy to simply walk openly into another Wendigo's territory," he said, coming close enough to talk.

"It's a common enough occurrence in populated areas," I replied. Beside me, Shadow started to growl at the approaching Wendigo. I set a hand on the dog's head and pet him, calming him down.

"*Only* if the trespasser is merely passing through," the other stated, stopping and regarding me steadily. I noticed that he stopped out of easy lunging range of the dogs. Not completely reckless, then.

"We are," I replied. "But the situation of your territory is... interesting. We were wondering why the locals were so shy."

The other Wendigo glanced at the humans with me. They were remaining quiet, leaving the discussion to us, though I knew Amica, at least, would still have her weapon out and up, ready to use. Lena likely had her knife ready, as well. Andrew… well, as long as he didn't look too much like a wounded fawn, he would be doing as much as he could.

"You travel with *humans*?" the Wendigo asked.

"For now. I need one for something, and the other two are… strays we picked up."

"Strays?" He smiled, a rather unpleasant expression. "Are you going to offer me any? That one looks like he's on his last leg, anyway."

"No, I'm not," I replied calmly. "They aren't for eating. The one I need doesn't want the other two dead, and how do you know the wounded one's not the one I need, anyway?"

"Need for what? What could *he* possibly do for you?"

I turned to look back at Andrew. Well… the stranger had a point. As Andrew was, he didn't appear to be very useful. Of course, Amica's usefulness to me was based on her knowledge, not on what she could do, though she was quite capable of handling herself. There was no reason Andrew couldn't know something I needed.

I turned back and shrugged. "It doesn't matter. None of them are available for eating."

"That's a pity," the other said. "I was thinking of just letting you go on your way, but I suppose I should make *some* sort of example of you."

I raised a brow. "What do you have to back up that threat?s"

He turned and pointed toward the building he had come from, up at the third-story windows. In two of the windows I could see the glinting of guns, no doubt wielded by those humans he took on as his personal lackeys.

120

I looked back at him. "Is there a purpose to this?"

"Of course. I have to protect the citizens from outsiders, after all. Although…" He looked toward where the local woman had fled. "I may have to clean up a loose end later. It's alright, I was hungry anyway."

"Let me make you a proposal," I said.

He raised a brow.

"Call off your humans, fight me yourself. Mine will stay out of it. If you want to look like you're the big savior of this territory, you'll look much better defeating me yourself than simply having your chattel shoot us." We didn't stand much of a chance if he simply had us shot where we stood. I just had to hope that this Wendigo's ego would be great enough that he would consider a fight with me to be an easy win.

He looked me over, obviously sizing me up. I was a bit shorter than him, though it would be hard to tell how muscled I may be underneath the coat I was wearing. The fact that I willingly associated with humans, and needed something from one of them that I apparently couldn't get myself, likely made me look fairly weak. Or at least, I hoped it did.

Never mind that he apparently used humans, himself, to back up his authority.

"Fine," he said, smirking. He made a gesture toward the gunmen, and I glanced up to see them retreating from the windows. "We will fight. You dogs will stay out of it, as will your humans. Mine will also remain out of the way. We will fight until death or submission, and then death to the loser."

I nodded. "That is acceptable."

"That is most definitely not acceptable!" Amica snapped from behind me.

I looked back at her. "The alternative is all of us being shot."

She scowled at me, not backing down for a long moment, then finally huffed and lowered her gun. "Fine," she said. "Kick his ass."

I looked over at Lena, who slowly returned her knife to its sheath at her belt. "Alright."

I smiled and winked. Turning to the dogs, I firmly indicated to them to stay, hoping they would understand and listen. I wasn't sure they would stay out of it once the fight began, but there wasn't much else I could do aside from tying them up, and I wasn't going to do that.

Turning, I stepped up to the resident Wendigo.

We squared up in the center of the road. My party remained back, out of the way. I wasn't sure where the other Wendigo's lackeys were now, but as long as they didn't shoot anyone, I didn't particularly care.

We circled each other, each sizing up the other. I already knew my opponent was taller than me, and that he had a sizeable level of self-assurance. He was confident enough in his own abilities that he had accepted my challenge rather than simply having me shot, and he *was* wearing an Enforcer's uniform, indicating that he had either been one, or had killed one at some point.

Of course, perhaps it was his pride more than his skill that had prompted him to take out the challenger himself, rather than leave me to the Normals.

He darted to the side, and I matched his movement, watching him closely. Shifting to a forward lunge, he tried to rake at my side with long, sharp nails. I jumped back, a plume of snow rising up behind me, avoiding his strike.

He wasn't trying to seriously injure, not yet. He was testing me, and I him.

I leaned back into a crouch with my backward momentum and pushed off from there. I stepped quickly forward and to the side, spinning and aiming a sweeping kick at his legs.

He evaded me by backing up, but, I noted, not quite as quickly as I had. With a snarl, he lunged forward again, meeting me in a grapple. We struggled against each other, judging each other's strength as we had each other's speed.

I was being pushed back, his superior weight forcing me to step backward to avoid being toppled over. Snarling myself, I released the grapple, ducking down and to the side and letting him stumble forward before catching himself.

He was stronger. I was faster. But who between us was smarter?

We continued for several minutes, him seeking an opening to close with me, me seeking to keep a distance between us. I would have to close with him eventually to deal any actual damage, but it had to be on my terms. I had to get in and out before he could get a good grip on me.

I just had to find a proper opening.

He lunged forward, but overstepped as I stepped aside, leaving himself open. I closed the distance, bringing my fists up to pound down on his exposed back.

With a quick twist around, he managed to catch my hands, snarling, and redirected them to the side, throwing me off balance.

He followed the momentum, pushing me to the ground on my stomach and coming down heavily with his knees on his back. His hands still gripped mine, and there wasn't much I could do with my face in the snow. I went limp, waiting.

I felt his hot breath on the back of my neck as he prepared to bite the back of my neck, to send large, sharp teeth tearing through the flesh and nerves. "I'm going to kill them all," he proclaimed. "Nice and slow. Think I might give you a slow death, too. Let you watch me flay them. Or maybe not."

I bucked, throwing my weight up and to the side, turning and bringing my arms around over my head so that I was facing him. I nearly dislocated my already-wounded shoulder, but my gambit succeeded. He was surprised by my sudden movement, though he retained his grip on my hands, leaving my arms crossed. I could work with that.

Turning my hands to change the angle of my wrists, I threw both arms out to my sides, crossing his arms and breaking his hold. My shoulder screamed in agony.

I sprang onto him, driving him down into the snow, my hands around his neck. He scrambled to break free, clawing viciously at my face with his nails, leaving long, bloody divots. I let my hunger overcome my pain, giving me strength, and dug my thumbs into his windpipe, my own nails puncturing his throat.

He gurgled something that would likely have been a scream if he could draw breath. I tightened my grip, digging my nails into the flesh of his neck. After several moments, he stopped struggling, and after a few more, I pulled my hands free.

"Don't gloat until you're finished," I said. My hands were covered in his blood, and my face with my own. I was in pain, and my hunger rivalled it as an empty, roaring hole in my stomach and head.

It took a moment for the sound of cheering to register with my senses. I turned, seeing Amica, Lena, and Andrew cheering my win. Seeing me look their way, Ash and Shadow rushed over and crowded against me with many licks and heavily-wagging tails as they picked up on the humans' excitement, distracting me for a moment from my hunger.

A gunshot went off, bringing searing pain an instant later. I fell, my leg deciding it didn't want to bear my weight. Around me, I heard sudden commotion. More gunshots were fired, someone screamed, people were running around, in front of, and behind me. Blood dripped from the gashes on my face into my eyes, making it difficult to see what was happening.

My leg hurt. My face and shoulder hurt. The pain mixed with my hunger, producing a cold, hungry rage. I needed to stand, needed to kill, to eat, to survive.

The gunshots fell silent. I stood, forcing my wounded leg to hold me enough to retain my balance, my vision still obscured by my own blood.

My sight and smell were compromised, but I could still hear. I shut my eyes, turning my head back and forth to catch the sounds around me and form a mental picture of the scene. One... two... four bodies moving around. Two four-legged, two two-legged. Two human. Food. One human remaining still, breathing heavily, sitting.

I started toward the weak one, the one sitting. I limped heavily on my bad leg, but the desire for food overrode the registering of pain. I could hear my prey shuffling backward, trying to escape me. Oh, that would do them no good. Not if they didn't *run*.

Another human was coming closer, but I paid them hardly any heed. If they came close enough to do anything, I would eat them too. Two would fill me more than one.

Something heavy struck my leg where I had been shot. I tried to turn, howling as the pain broke through my hunger, but my leg buckled again beneath me and I fell. My ears rang as the pain overloaded my senses, and I lost my focus on the events around me.

I roared in anger and hunger, trying once more to stand, but this time my leg would not support me and I fell once more into the snow. Blinking viciously, I managed to clear my vision enough to see the shapes of those around me. Close by, behind me now, was the weak one. In front of me was another human, at first appearing extremely deformed, but then I recognized that they were dragging something toward me. Beyond them, a third human was grappling with two four-legged shapes.

I tried to use my good leg to lunge forward, but the second human gave a great heave of their load and brought it between me and them. I snarled and started to claw over it, but my nails sank into soft, warm flesh, making me pause.

The smell filtered through the smell of my own blood, and I realized what was before me. A fourth human, this one already dead.

Well, whether they were alive or dead made no difference.

Chapter 11

I was warm when I awoke, nearly uncomfortably so. It was dark, and quiet, and my face felt as though it were made of a thick layer of very painful marshmallow. My leg ached, my shoulder as well, and for a long time I just lay there, contemplating how much I hurt. It struck me as odd that I was simultaneously in pain, and warm and comfortable.

I turned my head, looking around as well as I could through swollen eyelids. There was just enough light to make out the room, and to tell me that my eyes weren't completely swollen shut. Sitting up, I considered my surroundings and what I could last remember.

The last thing I could remember was hunger.

Since I had first regained control of myself after being changed, there were only three times I had lost control quite to that degree. The first was after my family wrote off my missing brother as a lost cause and I disregarded my own needs for the sake of searching for him. The second was after defending my territory against a challenging Wendigo and her two dogs and *very* narrowly succeeding. I started getting dogs of my own after that. And the third... well, I had just added it to my list.

I was well within the limits of my control now, though, so I must have eaten, and eaten well. In fact, my stomach was still slightly distended, so I couldn't have been unconscious for more than a day.

I sat up, carefully swinging my legs around over the side of the bed I found myself in. Yes, it *was* a bed... Another oddity.

One leg of my pants had been cut off, and my wounded leg bandaged. I considered it for a moment, trying to remember how I had been wounded, and failed for a moment to remember anything beyond the sound of gunfire before I hit a wall of remembered hunger.

So someone had shot me... Right. Just after I killed the Wendigo claiming this town. Which is when my face was injured. That figured out, I carefully stood, intending to go figure out what had happened after I stopped processing coherent thoughts. Thankfully, my leg would take some weight, and I was able to walk on my own, albeit slowly.

Opening the door, I found myself facing a hallway. The room I woke in was near the end of the hall. A window at the very end of the hall, to my right, showed that it was well past sunset.

Looking down the hall in the other direction, I saw the flickering glow of candlelight. I started in that direction.

The hall opened into a kitchen and dining room, lit by several mismatched candles sitting out on the table. Amica was sitting there, a mug clasped between her hands. It smelled like coffee.

She looked up as I approached, watching me. "Didn't think you'd be up so soon," she said.

I pulled out a chair and sat down heavily. "What was the damage?"

"You won. Got your face torn up, though."

I grunted. I knew that.

"That Wendigo's lackeys didn't like that you won, so they shot you. You didn't take it well."

I waited silently for her to continue. I didn't really fancy a lot of talking; it hurt to open my mouth and stretch the torn skin.

"I went after the lackeys, shot them before they could do any more damage, and the dogs went a little nuts and went after the ones that came out of the building at us. You went after Andrew."

"Are the dogs alright?" I broke in.

"Yeah, they're fine. I had to restrain them though, after the lackeys were killed. They wanted to help you, and we couldn't let them or you kill Andrew."

It seemed to me that, as many times as I nearly had already, it would be easier to just finish the job and stop us from having to worry about him. I refrained from stating that out loud.

"Lena hit your injured leg with the handle of her knife, which crippled you long enough for her to drag one of the dead lackeys over. Afterward…" she fell silent for a moment. Perhaps the thought of what I could do, did do, and could have done was a bit… unnerving. Most Normals certainly didn't take the reality of what Wendigos did very well.

"…we brought you here," Amica finished. "It's that woman's house, the one you ran down before everything went to Hell. Her name's Stacy. It took a bit of convincing for her to allow you to be brought in, but after assuring her that you wouldn't hurt anyone after you'd eaten, she allowed it."

I must have been very solidly unconscious if I hadn't woken up while they did that. Unless Lena happened to have some sort of tranquilizer in her pack. That… honestly wasn't unlikely.

"And what is Stacy going to think of me now?" I asked.

Amica looked me over. "Your leg barely holds your weight, your face is swollen and full of stitches, and your shoulder is still weak from where *I* shot you the other day. You're not going to be hunting anyone down for a day or two at least."

Well… she was correct, as much as I didn't want to admit it. Ironically enough, I was about as mobile as Andrew with his injured leg. I would heal more quickly, of course, but for now… we weren't traveling anywhere.

"Where are the dogs now?" I asked.

"Stacy wouldn't let them inside, she's allergic. She has a shed she set up with some old blankets for them, so they should be fine."

I considered going out to check on them immediately, but decided against that. That would require walking outside, through the snow, and I wanted to give my leg a few more hours rest before attempting that. They were likely sleeping, anyway, curled together in the darkness.

"You care a lot for them, don't you?" Amica asked, regarding me. The candlelight flickered across her face, making it a bit difficult to read her expression.

"They're good dogs," I replied, shrugging my good shoulder. "They pick up cues well, and I haven't had any problems with them. They're loyal and like me, and I like them."

She raised a brow, taking a sip of her coffee. "You care more about dogs than people."

"People are food." People cared about what you were. Dogs didn't.

She shrugged, conceding that point. "Why don't more Wendigo work together? It would be easier for you, and probably less lonely."

"We're apex predators," I replied, perhaps a bit too quickly. It was something I had rationalized through many times. "We require a lot of food from a slowly-reproducing source. Were we to frequently band together, we would eventually overwhelm the numbers of any local human population, no matter how big. Look at this town. There was one Wendigo here, and he would have slaughtered the entire town within a few years. We tend to gravitate toward cities because that's where the largest populations are. They can sustain us for longer, or indefinitely if we can gain a territory large enough in an affluent enough area."

"Somewhere where the population's still breeding," Amica said.

I nodded.

"What do you think the reasoning behind the pack back home is?" she asked.

"I don't know. Something must be going on between them and the government. Otherwise, they would have been eradicated as an unreasonable threat long ago."

Amica scowled. "If only."

I didn't reply. If the pack had been eradicated as soon as they came together, then perhaps Amica's daughter wouldn't have been killed. There was no certainty, of course, because there was no saying whether something or someone else wouldn't have killed her, but there was that chance.

Of course, if that territory had been freed, perhaps I would have ended up taking over it. The population was certainly denser and wealthier than in my own territory. Perhaps I would have been the one to kill her daughter.

I certainly wasn't going to voice that thought.

We lapsed into silence, the candles slowly burning lower, lighting the room with their warm, flickering glow. I liked candles. They weren't as harsh on my eyes as electric lights, and even unscented ones had a distinctive fire and wax smell that I found rather enjoyable.

After several minutes, I realized that it was odd that Amica was still up. "Are you going to sleep?" I asked.

"I'm taking the night watch," she said. "Stacy actually has some instant coffee left. I haven't had coffee in... a year at least. I'll go get some sleep in a few hours. We aren't going anywhere for a couple of days, anyway."

"You're up to watch for me?"

"Stacy insisted. She didn't want you roaming around unsupervised."

"Hmph." It made sense, though, and I wasn't offended. Her having me in the house was much like taking in a mountain lion. You wouldn't let one of those roam around as they pleased.

I leaned back in the chair. I was weary. Healing took a lot of energy, and I had been heavily injured multiple times in the past several days, and traveled a lot during that time. Even a Wendigo's body had limits. I really should go back to sleep, but that would mean standing back up and walking back down the hall. I didn't want to do that yet.

"You should go sleep," Amica commented, echoing my thoughts.

"Not yet," I replied. "I'll stay up a few more minutes, keep you company."

"Thanks."

I couldn't tell whether she was being sarcastic or sincere.

We remained in silence for several more minutes. Finally, after nearly dozing off in the chair, I accepted the fact that I was going to have to stand up. I did so, grimacing as I did.

"Make sure you get some sleep as well," I advised Amica.

She nodded. "Heal up and then we'll go look for your brother."

"Still up for that, huh?"

"Of course. We made a deal."

It was my turn to nod. We had. I still wasn't sure how we would take down the pack, but we would figure out something. Slowly, I walked back down the hallway, away from the candlelight, and into the bedroom in which I had awoken. Allowing myself a quiet groan as I lay down, I made myself as comfortable as I could and soon fell asleep.

It was light out when I awoke. Wan sunlight filtered in through the window, barely managing to shine through a thin layer of clouds. I ached less than the night before, but I felt stiff. My face was a little less puffy, and I felt gently around it, feeling stitches closing the deepest gashes. I would bear some rather prominent scars once those gashes healed up, but that didn't really bother me. Maybe it would make me look tougher, and would discourage challengers in the future. Provided I eventually made it back to my territory.

Standing, I stretched, carefully working through the stiffness of healing muscles and tendons. I wasn't ready for traveling yet, but I had some small level of mobility back.

I went out to the kitchen, drawing the gazes of everyone there. Lena nodded a greeting, while Andrew refused to look directly at me. The woman I had approached before, Stacy, regarded me with a steady, wary gaze. Apparently Amica had eventually gone to bed, as she was nowhere to be seen.

I looked around the room, then at Stacy. "Where's the door? I should check on my dogs."

She seemed a bit surprised at my request, but pointed in the proper direction. "The shed's around the corner to the left," she said.

"Thank you."

I went outside, stepping out into the snow. I wasn't wearing my coat, and one of my pant legs was missing, but the cold wouldn't bother me for how long I would be out here. I walked to the left, where Stacy had indicated the shed would be. Moving through the snow was difficult and somewhat painful, but I kept going.

The shed was just around the corner of the house. The door had been left partially open, no doubt so the dogs could get in and out. As I approached, I heard movement from inside, then both dogs came running out at me, jumping up excitedly. I braced myself as they approached, but they still managed to throw me off balance, knocking me down into the snow. The fall jarred my leg and shoulder, but I ignored the pain in favor of reassuring the dogs, who were blanketing me with licks while quietly whining in excitement.

I let this continue for a few moments, then shooed them off and away enough for me to stand. They were reluctant at first, but obeyed, tails still wagging cheerfully as I stood.

I spent several minutes petting the dogs, reassuring them that I was alright. Finally, I started back toward the house, telling the dogs to remain at the shed. After a few tries, they stopped attempting to follow me and remained. They would be fine out here. They could go out and run if they wanted to, and would be able to find some sort of food on their own.

Inside was mildly warmer than outside, and though the cold wasn't as much of a threat to me as to a Normal, it had seeped into my leg, making the wound ache jarringly.

"Are you alright?" Lena asked as I re-entered the kitchen, my limp more pronounced.

I nodded and sat in a vacant chair beside Andrew. He shied away a little as I sat down, but I pretended not to notice.

Stacy was watching me closely, scrutinizing my every move. I wasn't sure if she thought I was going to attack everyone, or if she was simply curious. I suspected the former, especially considering the likely-horrific state of my face.

I turned and matched her gaze, considering her. She was taller than I had first thought, but of course she would be when she wasn't cowering in the snow. Her long hair was pulled back in a ponytail, and she had a mug of that instant coffee. Looking around, I saw that everyone there did. She must be glad to have company, to use up that much of it.

"Are you, uh, feeling any better?" Stacy asked hesitantly. She probably shouldn't be drinking that coffee, as nervous as she already seemed, but that wasn't really my business.

"Yeah," I replied. "Thanks for the bed."

She shrugged, hands tight around her mug as if using it for support. "I couldn't just let you die out there, even if you are a... you know."

I raised a brow. "You seemed convinced earlier that we were going to kill you and everyone else in town as soon as we got the chance. What changed your mind?"

"I… wouldn't say my mind's been changed," she said slowly, looking away from me. "I still think you might be here to do that, but if you're not… well, I have a better chance to live if I side with you guys, right?"

That was a sensible argument, aside from the still believing we might be there to kill everyone. I shrugged. "It's a chance. We aren't staying here long. I'm sure Enforcers will come in and take over as soon as they realize the command of the town's shifted, which they'll hear about after the next supply truck comes through." I frowned at that thought. "When *is* the next supply truck coming through?"

"Three days."

That was fortuitous. Long enough to give me a chance to heal, but short enough not to make the residents too uncomfortable with my presence. I was, after all, an unknown appetite, and they didn't know how many I would kill to sate myself. They would be nervous, and nervous people acted irrationally.

I would make sure to keep the death toll low.

I turned to Lena. "Amica said there were two of the other Wendigo's lackeys killed. Did I eat both of them?"

She blinked in surprise at my question, and even Andrew looked up at me.

"No, just the one."

"Good. Don't dispose of the other body, if you haven't already. Just store it where it will freeze and stay fresh. I'll eat him later, rather than kill someone else."

Stacy swallowed, and when I glanced at her, her hands were shaking slightly. "You're… very cavalier about that," she said.

"About what? Eating? Why shouldn't I be? You don't get worked up about eating meat, do you?"

"My meat's not…"

"Human?"

"Sentient."

"Ahhh," I said, and shrugged. "I have to eat to live, same as you. My diet's just a little more restricted."

She didn't have anything to say to that.

Chapter 12

    Remaining in one place to heal was terribly frustrating. I wanted to be moving, to get closer to the information about my brother that I knew was waiting just beyond my reach. Stacy had some books, but they weren't in genres I was particularly interested in and I couldn't bring myself to read through them. By midday, I was restless and irritable, which put everyone else on edge. Just before dusk, Stacy left.

    I wasn't sure where she went, but I left the house soon after, heading outside to check on the dogs, then going to where Lena told me the other dead lackey was hidden. The walk, slow as it was, did much for clearing my head.

    When I returned, there was a small stack of books on the table; ones much more to my liking. The humans were in the living room, playing Euchre by candlelight.

    "Stacy brought you some books," Lena said, looking over her shoulder at me. "You seemed antsy this afternoon."

    "Thanks," I replied, looking through the stack. I picked one and sat down in a kitchen chair, stretching out my leg so it would be a little more comfortable.

    I read by candlelight for a few hours, the light more than sufficient for my own eyes. After a while, the humans finished up their card game. Apparently they didn't feel the need to guard me anymore, as they all went to bed and left me alone in the kitchen. I read for a bit longer, then decided that it would be best if I, too, went to bed. I wasn't mentally tired; I had been sleeping more in the past few days than I usually did in a week, but I was weary. The more I slept now, the faster I would regain my strength, and the more prepared I would be for whatever came next. Setting the book aside, I headed back down the hall and to the bedroom I had woken up in the night before.

The next day was spent much as the one before. By the end of the day, I had gotten through the book I started the previous night, and had started on another. My leg was feeling much better, and after dark I went out on a short run with the dogs to test it. It still wasn't back to full strength, but at least it could hold up to some activity.

The gashes on my face were itching abominably, and I had to restrain myself from scratching at them and tearing the stitches back open. Lena thought she would be able to remove them the next morning.

After I returned from my run, we gathered in the kitchen to discuss and plan what we were all going to do next.

"According to Stacy," I began, "the supply truck will be here the day after tomorrow. Amica and I will need to figure out a way to get on it without being noticed, so we can get the rest of the way to Columbus."

"What about us?" Lena asked.

"You and Andrew can do what you want," I replied. "You don't have to come with us. My deal is with Amica, not you."

"I'm not going with him," Andrew piped up. "I've been nearly eaten enough times, I'm not traveling anywhere else with a Wendigo."

"You're free to stay here," Stacy said. "Not like the town's lacking space for people."

Andrew nodded acceptance of the offer.

Lena looked over at him, then back at Amica and me. "I would like to go with you," she said. "I have more medical knowledge than either of you, and I know Columbus. I used to live there."

"How long ago? Do you have any idea of the current social climate there?" I asked.

She shrugged. "It's been a few years. As far as current events go, I just know what we get as rumors from people who happened to run across our settlement, and what we could pry from the train guards, which wasn't a lot."

Well, having another pair of eyes would make keeping watch for trouble easier. Of course, I would have to watch out for two humans rather than one, but Amica had proven herself pretty competent at taking care of herself, and I was sure Lena was as well, so that shouldn't be too difficult .

"Alright," I said. "You're free to come along. Stacy, what kind of trucks do they use to bring supplies?"

"It's usually a convoy," she said slowly. She had gotten a little more comfortable with my presence over the last couple of days, but was still obviously nervous about direct conversation. "They're the government trucks, the ones with the cloth tops over the back."

"Who meets them and accepts the supplies?"

"Usually Earl's... um, the Wendigo who claimed this territory, usually his closest lackeys. He had them unload and sort everything, and then they would distribute it among the people." She paused, then added, "they weren't *bad* about it, though. They made sure everyone got what they were supposed to."

I frowned thoughtfully, a plan starting to take shape. "Who's going to accept the supplies now?" I asked.

140

She shrugged. "I don't know. With the heads gone, probably whoever gets there first. Word of their deaths has definitely gotten around."

"Yeah, especially since we just left... Earl," Amica chuckled at the name, "lying in the middle of the street. So if there's uncertainty about the partitioning of the goods, it's likely there'll be a bit of confusion and chaos in the unloading, won't there?"

It was like Amica was reading my thoughts.

"Probably," Stacy agreed slowly. "And I don't know if anyone will bring out the proper tribute. We do have to pay for the supplies; they aren't free. We usually make stuff for it, paintings and leather goods and things like that, and it's all taken to storage before the trucks arrive so it can be brought out and loaded up."

"So," I said, "we have a town of people who don't know whether they'll get their proper allotment of food and necessities, and Enforcers who might not get paid. I think that sounds like something we can work with."

I considered the matter for a moment. It wasn't a certainty that chaos would erupt on its own, but maybe we didn't have to just let things unfold naturally. "Lena," I said, "do you think you'd be up for spreading a little... dissention?"

"How so?" she asked.

"Just spread the idea that not everyone may be trustworthy with the supplies. You won't have to say much, the residents are probably already uncertain and anxious about their future."

Stacy frowned. "The Enforcers will have guns. If the people turn into a mob, a lot of them could be killed."

Yeah, but it would be easier to slip into a truck and hide with a riot as cover. "I doubt they'll actually riot," I lied, "and once the Enforcers realize something's up, they'll start taking measures to control the situation and will dole the supplies out themselves instead of leaving it to the townsfolk."

She didn't seem completely reassured. "Alright…" she said slowly. "I really don't like how nonchalant you are about people's *deaths*."

"Everyone's going to die eventually," I replied. "A bullet's usually better than the cold."

She didn't like that.

We all went our own ways after that. Amica grabbed out of the books from the stack Stacy had borrowed from a neighbor and retreated with it and a candle to the living room. I returned to my own book.

Andrew appeared to be playing solitaire, and Lena and Stacy retreated to another corner of the living room to discuss something. I didn't bother listening closely enough to hear what they were saying.

The next morning, Lena pulled out a small pair of shears and a set of tweezers from her bag, sat me down at the kitchen table, and proceeded to pull out my stitches. It didn't hurt much, but feeling the rigid threads pull through my skin and out was strange. From what I remembered of hospitals, they usually tried to use stitches that would dissolve away on their own, or else they would use glue that would break down on its own over time. These old fashioned stitches were probably saved only for the heavier jobs. We had to make do with what we had, though, and it was a good thing that Lena had her well-stocked pack.

"There," she said as she finished. She had been very quiet as she had taken them out, concentrating closely on her task. "I got all of them. Your face will itch for another day or two, and the scars will probably last a few years, but they're healing well. It's definitely a good thing you don't get infections. Who knows what that guy had under his fingernails."

"Actually," I began.

She shushed me. "I don't want to actually know," she said.

I chuckled at that.

Lena paused in putting her things away and looked back up at me. "That's a first," she said.

"What?"

"You laughing. You don't do it much."

I shrugged. It wasn't really something I thought about. I didn't usually have a lot of social interaction, so there wasn't really anyone to laugh with. Besides, large, sharp teeth bared while laughing didn't exactly reassure people.

"Let me see your leg," Lena said after a moment. "Put it up on the table here."

I did so, and she proceeded to unwind the bandage. The wound itself was more or less healed over. There was a little puckering around it where the skin had knit itself back together. Lena poked at and around it for a moment, and while it hurt a bit and the skin was tender, it wasn't unbearable.

"You can probably leave it un-bandaged now," she commented, "and you should probably get rid of the pants that are missing a leg. They're covered in blood, and that's not going to come out."

"Most of my clothes are bloodstained," I pointed out. Pretty much the only way to avoid that would be to hunt naked, and it was a little too cold this time of year for that, even for me.

She finished putting her stuff away, throwing the bandage out in the trash. "You feel up for heading out tomorrow?" she asked.

"Yeah, I'll be fine. A little sore still, but well enough."

Lena shook her head. "It's amazing how fast Wendigos heal. I remember when my husband would get hurt. He'd come home a bloody, torn-up mess, then a few days later he'd be fine, providing he got properly fed during that time. He... did usually try to do that *before* coming home."

"Probably a good idea," I replied.

"It's not you guys' fault," she countered. "It's just how you react to trauma. Humans go into shock, Wendigos..."

"Lose coherent thought and revert to basic predatory instinct?" I finished.

"Yes."

I shook my head. I still thought she was far too nonchalant about what I was, but hey, *she* wasn't the one whom I had nearly eaten multiple times in the past several days. Andrew, at least, was properly wary of me.

"How's Andrew's leg?" I asked.

"It had started to get infected," she replied. "Thankfully, we had enough time at the settlement before... before the raid for it to be properly cleaned out and bandaged, but it's difficult to get everything out of a wound like that. I gave him some antibiotics, and hopefully they'll actually work. Getting some rest and not having to walk on it is helping him a lot, though."

"That's good. I almost feel bad for nearly eating him so many times."

"You? Feel bad about almost killing someone?"

I wasn't *completely* heartless. "I feel bad because it's happened so many times," I replied. "I don't make a habit of *nearly* killing people, I either do or I don't. Almost doing it is just rude."

"Ahh," she said, sounding skeptical. "Right."

I shrugged and lowered my leg from the table. What she believed about me was beyond my control.

Lena returned her supplies to her backpack, and I went out to check on the dogs and make sure they would be ready to head out early tomorrow. We would have to be in position before the trucks arrived; somewhere out of sight but where we could easily move up to the convoy. After that, our window of opportunity all depended on the actions of the crowd, which we couldn't be sure of.

But nothing incites chaos like uncertainty and change.

The next day we ensured everything was packed and ready to go early. I took care of the last of the dead lackey, and made sure the dogs were fed and in good condition, double-checking that they had no cracked paws or mangled fur.

We left Stacy's around ten, an hour before the convoy was supposed to arrive. She didn't seem sad to see us go, but she wasn't cheerful about it, so I guessed that she liked the company more than she let on. Well, at least liked the human company. She didn't seem to think well of me.

There were already people milling around at the edges of the main street when we arrived. We stayed away from them, going mostly unnoticed. Those few who did take notice of us didn't say anything, just turned away nervously and acted like they hadn't seen us.

We took up our position by the same building Earl had stepped out of a few days ago, where we would have a good view of the street. The dogs lay down once they caught on that we weren't going anywhere for a while, their coats blending in with the shadows.

As we waited, more people came out to the main street. There were a surprising number of people left in this town, and apparently they all wanted to make sure they got their fair share of supplies.

A few skirmishes broke out among the residents, but overall the waiting was fairly peaceful, though cut by an underlying level of tension. It was likely most of them knew each other, had even grown up together. I wondered how much of that would matter when faced with the potential of starvation, as was the fate of so many towns when government supply chains dried up.

I heard the trucks before we could see them, the sound carrying over the snowy fields around the town. The crowd stirred, shifting nervously like small birds disturbed by a strange sound, but not disturbed enough to fly away and leave the promise of food behind.

I wasn't sure what the Enforcers would think of finding this many people waiting here for them. Certainly Earl never allowed this many people out here to meet the outsiders. All the better for his closest lackeys to skim a little off the top of the delivery, I was sure, despite Stacy's insistence that they were fair with the apportioning.

The trucks rumbled in, preceded by two large plows sending out large plumes of snow on either side of the road,

146

adding to the piles lining the stretch. The crowd moved back, a few exclamations heard over the sound of the vehicles, but quickly pushed forward again, lining the top of the snow-piles and gradually pressing down closer to the road itself.

The trucks stopped, but were not turned off. The Enforcers seemed uncomfortable with the crowd, unwilling to leave themselves without an easy means of escape should it be necessary.

After several long moments of uneasy silence, a truck-door opened. A man stepped out, dressed in bulky, cold-worthy clothes that likely concealed bullet-proof layers underneath. A semi-automatic gun was strapped to one hip, and a long machete to the other. A heavy hand-gun was gripped in one hand. As he stepped out, he gazed on the gathered residents, frowning.

"Where's the guys in charge?" he asked loudly, voice carrying even above the sound of the trucks.

For a long moment, no one replied, until someone dared yell out: "they're dead!" A cautious smatter of cheers met this exclamation.

The Enforcer's frown deepened, and he motioned his men from the trucks. They stepped out and down, joining him, though one person remained in each truck at the steering wheel. The plow drivers also remained in their vehicles, ready to move forward if commanded.

"Alright," the head Enforcer called, "here's how this is going down. We're going to unload the allotted cargo, and you will bring out the appropriate payment. Once everything is unloaded and loaded, we'll leave, and you can go back to whatever miserable things you do in this frozen Hell of a town. Capiche?"

There was some murmuring and shifting from the crowd, but no one spoke up.

"Good," he stated. He turned to his men and started directing them, keeping three with him while the rest went to unload the trucks. The crowd milled and buzzed with low conversation for a few moments before a sizable group of people left, presumably to retrieve the goods set aside as payment for the supply shipment.

We waited tensely, watching the whole thing unfold. We wouldn't be able to make a dash to the trucks unless there was some sort of distraction. Ideally, the crowd would occupy the Enforcers' attention long enough for us to drive one of the trucks away ourselves, but in lieu of that, we could always just hide in the back.

But our plan did hinge on the actions of the crowd.

"We may need to instigate some chaos," I murmured, glancing away from the crowd and back to the two humans beside me.

Lena frowned. "I'm not sure that's a good idea. I've seen food riots. They aren't pretty."

"No," I replied, "but they sure as hell are distracting."

"Cover your ears," Amica said from behind me, and I didn't have more than that warning before she raised a hand, holding up her gun and shooting into the sky.

The effect was instantaneous. The crowd erupted into movement, shouts rising up over the ringing in my ears. They surged toward the Enforcers, who in turn pulled up their weapons, and soon, the sound of several other gunshots joined the first.

148

"That'll work," I said, though I didn't think anyone actually heard me. My ears were painfully ringing from the shot, and the chaos would obscure any attempt at normal conversation. Ash had yelped and run from our hiding place at the initial gunshot, but was now frozen in place between us and the trucks, torn between the gun sound behind her, and the many gunshots ahead.

I didn't leave her deliberating for long. Seizing our opportunity, I sprung forward, covering the distance between the alcove and the nearest truck as quickly as I could, though with my injured leg the other two were able to easily catch up and keep pace. Ash joined us as we passed her, loping alongside Shadow.

I went to the back of a truck at the rear of the short convoy. Commotion reigned nearby, bullets occasionally whizzing by us, leaving a couple holes in the canvas canopy of the truck.

I peeked around the corner, gauging the commotion and whether we could chance simply stealing the truck and leaving.

I decided I didn't want to risk it. Back here was relatively quiet, with less direct commotion, and taking out the driver may draw attention.

Ducking back behind the truck, I gestured up and into it. The others nodded. Lena climbed in while Amica covered us, gun out. I handed each dog up to Lena, then climbed in myself, Amica following close behind.

The sound of the rioting outside was barely dampened by the canvas. We kept low and moved toward the cab, trying both to keep out of the way of stray bullets and to keep from rocking the truck and alerting the driver.

There were still several crates in the truck bed, some covered with tarps. Some were full, most were empty. Apparently the Government considered the metal crates a valuable enough commodity not to leave them behind at the random backwater towns that needed regular supplying.

This, of course, simply supplied us with additional cover.

Normally, the Enforcers would thoroughly check their cargo before leaving a town, ensuring that no locals had stowed away just as we were doing, tucking themselves within crates and beneath tarps. This time, however, as soon as the mob started to quiet down, demoralized enough by injury and fear to scatter, the convoy started off, the remaining Enforcers cutting their losses and leaving, payment pick-up and supply drop-off be damned.

The plows ahead cleared the way, and the convoy moved out, quickly leaving the small town behind.

I looked out through the back of the truck as we rode away. The main street snow was stained red and a few stragglers were still shouting after the departing vehicles. Sighing, I sank down, leaning back against a crate. We had left a lot of death behind us. I felt a little bad that this was how things had turned out.

Still, we were out and on our way, and I was one step closer to discovering my brother's fate.

Chapter 13

The trucks didn't make fast progress. They were paced to the plows ahead, which had to clear away several inches of snow in front of the trucks' passage. We didn't speak, not wanting to catch the attention of the Enforcers in the cab, separated from us only by a layer of canvas and a pane of glass. Not that anyone seemed in the talking mood, anyway. It hadn't been a particularly glamorous get-away, and I was fairly certain that the deaths left behind us were weighing heavily on everyone's minds.

After just sitting there became boring, I turned my thoughts to what we were going to do next. After the injuries and, possibly, casualties they had sustained at the last stop, it was likely the Enforcers would return directly to the nearest city, our destination. Once we stopped, we were going to have to make a run for it, no matter where in Columbus that was. Being at the back of the convoy, it was possible that we could get away unseen, but it was also likely that we were heading for a fenced-in compound, in which case we would have to bail before the trucks actually entered. Given the slow speed of the convoy, though, jumping wouldn't be terribly risky, especially now that Andrew wasn't slowing us down.

As we continued to ride, I found myself running out of things I was comfortable thinking about and instead occupied myself by watching the snow and snow-covered trees pass by out of the open back of the truck bed. The dogs curled up beside me and fell asleep, comfortable with the ride.

A change in the ambient sounds around us brought me out of a doze. The ever-present rumble of the truck's engine had disappeared, leaving an eerie quiet around us. I looked around, meeting the gaze of the others as they roused from their own slumber.

The trucks had arrived at their destination, and we needed to leave. Quickly.

"We're going to have to run before they start unloading," I whispered as the situation registered, standing and moving carefully to the rear of the truck. I could hear the others shifting to follow me, the dogs' nails scrabbling uncomfortably loudly on the metal floor. Outside, we could hear the crunching of snow under soldiers' feet.

I glanced back at the others, who nodded their readiness, then turned and leapt from the back of the truck, the dogs on my heels and the women close after. Behind us, someone began shouting.

I burst into sunlight, nearly blinded by the glare off the snow. I didn't pause to look behind me, knowing the others would follow and hoping that no one would be shot down by the Enforcers. We were in what looked like an old parking lot, surrounded by fencing. It was nearly clear of snow, except for huge piles pushed to the corners of the fenced-in space. The rest of the area was largely taken up by parked vehicles: large trucks and jeeps, both civilian and military grade.

Thankfully, these parked vehicles gave us some cover. I had just ducked behind the nearest, the pounding footsteps of the others close behind me, when I heard the first gunshots ping loudly off the metal of the truck. I dashed out of my hiding place and to the next truck, taking cover again before looking for my next opening and continuing on. Luckily, Ash didn't bolt this time and instead stuck close to me.

The five of us continued until we reached one of the snow mounds. More Enforcers had been called in and were running after us, firing shots that sent up sprays of snow to either side.

We couldn't climb the snow directly; we would be picked off as soon as we got out into the open. We couldn't vault over the fence, either. It was too tall for that, designed to keep trespassers out.

I balked for a moment, before another gunshot rang out nearby. We needed a distraction. Turning, I tapped Amica and Lena's shoulders and pointed toward the snow mountain, then ran back the way we came, toward the Enforcers. I could only hope they took advantage of my diversion. The dogs followed me, though I wished they had gone with Amica and Lena. Nothing for it now, though.

Shouting followed my movements as I ducked out from behind one truck, running across to another. Bullets zipped by, just behind me. Behind the new truck, I turned, taking in the situation. At least a quarter of the Enforcers were still going after the others. I needed to get the attention of *all* of them.

As a man turned the corner around the truck, I leapt, barreling into him. We crashed into the snow and the dogs followed my example, attacking with flashing teeth. I jumped back up and kept moving, pushing straight through a group of several Enforcers who yelled with surprise when they saw me. My mouth was bloodied, the man behind me laying on the snow with his throat torn open, bleeding out.

That got their attention. The cry went up to go after the Wendigo, and the dogs and I ran. I knew we couldn't dodge bullets for long. Our luck was going to quickly run out.

I recognized the convoy we came in on by the fresh tire tracks. This time when I ducked around the truck, I wrenched open the door and clambered in, calling in the dogs with me. I slammed the door shut, glad to find what I suspected would be true. The keys were still in the ignition.

The fact that I didn't reappear from behind the truck seemed to puzzle the Enforcers, and for that brief moment the gunfire stopped.

In the silence, the truck's engine roared to life. I put it into drive and stomped on the gas, sending it lurching forward. In front of me, two Enforcers jumped out of the way, though several others came in from the sides, guns raised to shoot. I ignored the sound of bullets hitting the vehicle, steering between rows of parked trucks to get back to the mound of plowed snow. If I could just make it that far...

The driver-side window shattered into a crystalline multitude of pieces as a bullet angled through it. It passed back out through the windshield, leaving a second hole, surrounded by spider-web cracks. I kept driving.

At the mount, I continued forward. I threw the door open while the truck was still moving and shifted it into neutral, letting the momentum of the truck carry it to the top. I leapt out, Ash and Shadow close behind me. Behind us, the truck offered some scant cover as it started rolling backward down the mountain of snow, back toward the pursuing Enforcers. We leapt over the fence and ran toward the street and buildings beyond. I couldn't see Amica or Lena anywhere. They had likely taken cover in an abandoned building. I could have the

154

dogs track them down later, assuming we got away from the Enforcers.

A few more gunshots blew chips of asphalt from the street nearby, but it seemed that the Enforcers weren't terribly keen on continuing the pursuit outside their fenced lot.

I ducked through an open doorway, the dogs close behind me, and slumped down against the wall, out of sight from the door or any windows. I would give the dogs and myself a few minutes to rest and catch our breath, then go in search of Amica and Lena. Their tracks should be visible somewhere, and the dogs could track them from there.

Once I was satisfied the dogs were rested enough to continue, I left the shelter of the dilapidated house to go seek out the others.

I had to circle back out to the front of the house, in plain sight of the Enforcers' lot, to find the start of their trail. I found the tracks quickly, though, and followed them away from the Enforcers, between two houses and into the neighborhood beyond.

The tracks stopped at the far end of the block at the edge of a cleared street. Amica and Lena had apparently taken advantage of the lack of snow to obscure their trail, as it didn't continue directly on the other side.

I went back to where the tracks ended, crouched, and called the dogs over, indicating the footprints. They followed my hand, sniffing curiously, then seemed to catch the gist and headed off down the road. I could only hope they were actually following the scent I wanted.

After a few minutes of walking, the dogs veered off the road, heading back toward the parking lot. They led me up to a house with all but one of its windows boarded, its vinyl siding yellowed and cracked. The door was shut, but opened with a turn of the knob.

As I entered, I was met with the sight of Amica holding a heavy length of pipe, and Lena a board, both ready to bring them down on my head. Once they recognized me, however, they lowered their improvised weapons and stepped back.

I closed the door behind me and the dogs, locking it from the inside. We wouldn't be able to stay here long, the Enforcers may choose to search for us, but it would be secure enough for now.

"You alright?" Amica asked, peeking out of a crack in a boarded-up window to make sure no one was behind me.

I nodded. "Their aim wasn't great. I don't think they followed me, but we should move on soon. Do either of you know where in the city we are?"

Lena frowned, thinking, then shook her head. "No. We're probably on the western outskirts, just judging by the direction we came from. We'll need to hit a major road to know for certain."

"We can head east until we hit something," Amica said.

"That would probably be our best bet," I agreed. I looked around at what had once been a decent-sized living room. The carpet still held some dimples from where the couch must have been. The furniture had all been removed, indicating that the inhabitants had successfully moved away instead of simply fled or died, though a few pieces of trash and a small, once-bright-blue teddy bear sitting in a corner indicated that they also left in a hurry.

"I wonder what happened to this neighborhood," Lena mused, likely coming to a similar conclusion.

156

I shrugged. "The Enforcers may have cleared it out to decrease the area of land they had to protect. Or maybe there was a Wendigo outbreak here and they left to protect themselves. We can't really know at this point."

"We haven't been elsewhere in the house yet. They may have left other things behind," Lena commented, turning her gaze to a doorway that likely led to the kitchen.

Amica nodded. "You look in the kitchen, I'll look for a basement and see if anything's there."

"What are you hoping to find?" I asked, following Amica deeper into the house.

"Food," Amica replied.

Right. Food. They needed something other than... well...

I stayed above while she went into the basement, returning to the living room to keep an eye out for anyone approaching outside. There wasn't good visibility through the boarded windows, but I could see well enough.

I had only been keeping watch for a few minutes when I saw the first figure coming down the street, dressed in a dark military-issue uniform and carrying a rather large gun.

Turning away from the window, I went to the kitchen for Lena. "They're looking for us," I said, "we need to move on."

She closed the cupboard she had been looking through and shouldered her backpack, nodding and heading back to the living room.

On the way back, I stopped at the top of the basement stairs. "Amica, we need to go."

"Coming," she called up.

We gathered back in the living room, peering through gaps in the boarded windows. After several minutes of seeing no Enforcers, we headed out, slipping through the door and closing it behind us.

After passing by several blocks of abandoned houses, we finally began to see signs of habitation. The roads were snow-bound away from the Enforcer's lot, making the going slow, but it also made it obvious when we reached an inhabited neighborhood again.

I walked through the last few feet of snow to smooth path, the snow packed hard by many passing feet. The paths crisscrossed the snow-covered streets, uneven but easier to walk along than knee-deep, loose snow.

Despite the paths, most of the houses here still had boarded windows, looking as abandoned as those we had already passed. Behind us, the sun was beginning to set, shadows lengthening around us. No one was out walking, making this area almost more eerie than the abandoned neighborhood we just left.

"We should find somewhere to stay for the night," Lena said, breaking the silence.

I looked back at her, considering the suggestion. She was right, of course. We didn't want to travel in an unfamiliar area in the dark, and she and Amica would need to rest and eat. I may even do some hunting in the night, if I could verify that this territory didn't belong to another Wendigo.

"We'll use another abandoned house, one without any paths coming from it," Amica said, coming up to stand beside Lena.

That was sensible. I looked back to Lena. "Do you recognize where we are?" I asked.

She shook her head. "Not yet. We've just been walking through residential neighborhoods. I would guess we'll hit a major road soon, but I haven't seen one yet."

I didn't recognize where we were yet, either. I would have preferred to know where we were, and how far away I was from the files that would tell me of my brother's fate, but I nodded. There wasn't much I could do at the moment. "Alright. Shelter first."

We continued on for another block before we found a house we could be certain was empty. The front door was locked, and had a piece of paper nailed to it stating that trespassing was prohibited. It was unlikely we would be caught staying here for one night, though. The back door was also locked, but we found that one of the windows on the first floor had been broken through, the broken glass cleared away and a human-sized hole left in the boarding still partially covering it. Someone had been here at some point, but judging by the pristineness of the snow outside, they had not been here for quite some time.

I went in first, the dogs jumping up and scrabbling in behind me. I scanned the room beyond, my eyes quickly adapting to the gloom within. There was no one there.

"Clear," I said over my shoulder, moving further into the room and out of the way. Amica climbed in next, followed by Lena.

I continued deeper into the house as they climbed in. I wanted to be sure no one, and nothing, was here before settling down for the night. By the time I returned to the first room, the two humans had opened some canned food Amica had apparently found in the basement of the last house, standing as they ate to keep the dogs away from the food.

"You've been carrying those all day?" I asked Amica, surprised. Canned food was *heavy*.

She shrugged. "Having food's more important than having a sore back for a day or two."

Lena nodded, lifting her can in a seconding gesture. "Take food where you can find it," she said.

"I can't argue with that," I commented, calling the dogs to me and crossing back to the open window. Outside, the sun had nearly fully set, leaving us in deep gloom. "I'm going hunting."

The streets were silent, deserted at this hour. None of the streetlamps worked, leaving the once well-lit neighborhood dim. The sky was mostly clear though, a waxing moon just over half full shining down and illuminating the snow-covered city well enough for me to see. I wasn't actually planning to hunt just yet. A small amount of light still shone in the West, and I wanted it to be full dark before I set off after someone to eat. There was no reason to increase the risk of being caught at my task. For now, I was simply going to do a bit of reconnaissance.

I jogged down the street toward the east, following one of the conveniently well-trodden foot-paths. The dogs followed me, sometimes pacing out to either side, other times following directly behind, taking the easier path. They seemed happy to be out and traveling at a pace more suited for their loping gait than hours of walking.

It took less than half an hour for us to reach a larger street. The buildings had been drawing closer to each other for a few blocks until they formed proper alleys, while the road I was following opened out onto a larger, four-lane street. At the

160

corner, I paused and looked for a street sign, hoping one still remained. Making note of the street name, I looked around, noting my surroundings.

This road was kept clear, plowed regularly enough that black asphalt showed through in some places underneath slick, compacted snow. It didn't look particularly pleasant to drive down, but you would be able to, which meant that this was a main thoroughfare used by both Enforcers and those who still had the money to afford both a car and gas. I looked to my left, down the sidewalk, my gaze following the continuation of the well-trodden path I had followed to get here. It turned and went up to a building less than a block from where I stood, and judging by the compactness of the snow there, and the number of other paths leading to the same location, I surmised that the location was likely a distribution point; a place where Government officials and Enforcer teams brought relief supplies for those who couldn't get to a job or a place to actually buy those supplies.

Of course, the offerings at such locations were sparse and tended to lack anything more than basic nutrition; they were field rations at best, or left-overs of foods just old enough to be unsellable.

It wasn't a happy place. I looked away, to my right.

A bit of movement caught my attention. There were flickers of shadow and light playing out onto the street from an alleyway. Intrigued, I walked in that direction, Ash and Shadow close beside me.

I paused at the mouth of the alley. Peering around the corner, I could see more light, coming from what appeared to be an old backyard grill. Three people huddled around the small flames. I frowned at that sight. They were vulnerable out here, with no walls to shelter them from cold, Enforcer, or Wendigo. Why had they not taken refuge in an abandoned house?

I watched them for a few moments, then stepped forward, snow crunching under my feet. They looked up from their fire, taking in what they could see of my appearance and the two dogs at my heels. The dogs seemed to scare them more than I did. Perhaps they couldn't see enough of me beyond the glare of the firelight to identify me as a Wendigo?

For a moment, we stood in a strange tableau: Wendigo and hounds, and homeless, desperate humans. The silence was broken when one of them spoke.

"Care for a spot? Can't say we have much to offer, but the body heat of six's better than three."

His voice was rough. Perhaps he was older, or had smoked, back when tobacco was an easily-acquired commodity. Poor air flow. Low stamina, slow moving.

I stepped forward, closer to the light and the group. "Are you sure you want me to join you?" I asked, trying to get a feel for their attitudes toward me once I was identified. It would be good to know how people here reacted to the sight and presence of a Wendigo, and if they were, for some reason, willing to talk to me, it would be prudent to ask them for information on the local Enforcers.

The middle-aged man shrugged. "Nah, you're fine. 'S not like we're more liked than you." He laughed, a wheezy, pained sound that broke into a cough. I watched him, acutely aware of his weakness, of how easy it would be to kill him.

I pulled over an empty box and sat.

"What about you two?" I asked the others.

The one to my left shrugged, not looking away from the fire, her hands held close to the flames. Two of her fingertips were blackened with frostbite.

The third, sitting to my right, looked at me, eying me up and down. He was a relatively young man, probably in his mid to late twenties. "Nothing we can do if you do want to eat us," he said. "We may as well be polite food."

"Is there a resident Wendigo?" I asked.

The older man shook his head, laughing his wheezy laugh again. "Oh no. There 'aven't been any like you here for two years. The government came in, lured 'em all to the West, and released some sorta Hellfire on 'em. Didn't hurt the houses, but it dissolved any flesh it came in contact with. Ate through 'em, bones and all."

"That's not true," the younger man said. I looked at him, intrigued.

"Aint it?" the older asked.

"It's not," he insisted. He looked back up at me. "What *I* heard was that while there *was* a concerted hunt two years ago to eradicate them from the city, *that* was only the public story. *I* was told that there were some who the Government wanted to tame and turn into weapons. They let them live on the provision that they would only eat who the Government told them to. They all live downtown now, addicted to vat-grown meat and too lazy to leave their homes."

The older man scoffed. "Now why'n Hell would the Government leave any of 'em alive, no offense to yerself o'course," he nodded at me. "Tiger can't change its stripes, can't it?"

"They're still eating human meat," the younger countered. "It's just lab-grown, and laced with some sort of mind-control drug."

"Nah, they were all killed by flesh-eating gas."

I wasn't sure who to believe, if either. Even in the current state of the world, rumors spread quickly, and it was likely any number of explanations circulated around the lines at the food dispensary. Still, what I *could* take away from their stories was the fact that this territory did not have a resident Wendigo. That was one worry down.

"What about the Enforcers?" I asked. "What are they like here?"

"How far out'r you from?" the older man asked.

"Chicago," I replied.

"Wow," the younger said. "How did you get out here? Did you take the train?"

"I did."

"Hmph." The elder didn't seem impressed. "Trains. Never did like 'em. They derail too easily, get stuck in the snow. What we should do is use some of those feral dogs runnin' all over the place. Hook 'em up to sleds. That'll get people from one place to another faster than trains or trucks. They can just go right on over the snow."

I placed a hand on Ash's head appreciatively. She leaned in closer to me.

"Anyway," he continued, "the soldiers around here aren't nothin' to worry about, so long 's you stay out of property that's not yours. Can't say what they'd do to your sort. But they keep us fed, more or less. 'Nuff to keep us alive, anyway."

"Not any more than that, though," the young man chimed in again. "Sure, they don't shoot or beat anyone for being on

164

the streets, but they sure don't go out of their way to help us, either. With all the empty houses around, you'd think they'd make the landowners let us stay."

I looked over at the woman, who had a ragged blanket wrapped around her thin frame, unkempt hair trailing out from under a winter hat in small tufts. She still hadn't spoken.

"She doesn't talk," the young man said, following my gaze. "I haven't ever heard her say anything, at least. I think someone might have cut her tongue out."

The woman looked up, eying the young man, but continued to say nothing. After a moment, she looked back down at the fire, continuing to warm her hands.

"So the Enforcers allow people to live on the streets?" I asked.

"I don't know how they couldn't," the young man said. "There are enough of us without the money to keep our homes, and without families to take us in. They won't let us move back into the outer empty neighborhoods. So we just make do as well as we can."

This was all quite different from what I was used to, but different cities would be run differently, even if the national government was still the same. Each local division of Enforcers would have their own methods for dealing with their populous.

I stood. "Thank you for the information. Stay warm."

All three watched me as I stood, each of them tensing slightly at my movement. I smiled a little. So they weren't as nonchalant about my presence as they told themselves they were. Well, they were in no danger from me, tonight at least. Whether that was actually a better fate was debatable.

I turned, heading back up the alley to the street, and traced my steps back the way I came. If their words could be trusted, there would be more people out on the street tonight. There would likely be several near the dispensary, where they could get in line as quickly as possible to get their hands on the limited food supplies. It wouldn't be hard to find prey.

It was just past midnight when I returned to the deserted house, having fed and cleaned off the evidence of my meal. Amica was awake on watch when I returned, and she greeted me quietly before turning back to her vigil at the open window. The dogs made a fair amount of noise as they clambered in behind me, however, scrabbling claws not exactly built for climbing through windows, and the noise woke Lena.

Since they were both awake now, I told them what I had discovered. We would likely have easy traveling, so long as the Enforcers didn't take violent offense to me on sight.

"Given that there apparently aren't any Wendigos in the city," Lena mused, "they might react more violently than expected to keep it that way."

I frowned. That was a good point. Looking over the two humans, I considered our options. "We could travel at night," I suggested. They wouldn't be able to see as well, which would make our travel slower, and it would be colder, but we would be less likely to run into Enforcer patrols.

After a moment of silence, Amica spoke. "That wouldn't be terrible," she said, though she sounded somewhat reluctant.

"I would be willing to travel at night," Lena agreed.

"We should stay here through the day and head out tomorrow night," Amica said. "Rest up before we move out."

I wasn't particularly happy about this suggestion, wanting to be moving as soon as possible, but I had to admit it was a good idea. We had been walking for much of the day, and they needed some sleep. My leg twinged a bit, reminding me that *I* could use some rest as well.

"Might as well," Lena agreed, sitting where she could view the open window. "I'll take next watch. You two sleep."

<h1 style="text-align:center">Chapter 14</h1>

The night brought a cold snap, the fallen snow becoming crisp and hard beneath the clear sky. Though there was no heating in the abandoned house, the broken window was at least facing away from the wind, so it was somewhat warmer inside than outside. We spent the day in the house, listening to the rustling of bare branches outside and the occasional crunch of someone passing by. Apparently the emptiness of the streets yesterday evening wasn't always the case. Perhaps it was a food handout day. Perhaps the Enforcers came back from their rounds in the rural towns and generously handed out surplus tithes in their own city.

Yeah right.

Having eaten well during the night, I found myself more or less comfortable with waiting. Lena pulled out a deck of cards around noon, and she and Amica played a few rounds of some game I didn't recognize.

After watching them for a time, I moved closer, leaning against the wall as I observed their game.

"Do you want to join?" Lena asked.

I shook my head. "No, I'll just watch."

"Watching's no fun."

"It's plenty of fun," I countered. "I find it quite interesting, especially since I can see both of your hands."

Amica scowled at me. "No hints."

"I wouldn't ever think of cheating," I replied, smiling. "I'm just content to see how this plays out."

"Are you sure you don't want to play?" Lena asked again.

"Quite sure. I'm not really into card games."

She looked up, eying me quizzically. "What games are you into?"

I raised a brow at her question. It wasn't something I really thought of much anymore. "I liked RPGs, back when I had a computer or people to play them with."

"Ahh." She looked back down at her hand, laying a card face down on the floor before her. "My family would always play card games at reunions. Depending on the game, we could have eight or ten people playing at once. Canasta nights got really intense."

Amica glanced up briefly from her hand to eye Lena, her expression carefully neutral. "I can't say I remember ever attending a family reunion. I did have some board games I played with my daughter, but I haven't touched them since..." She trailed off, placing a card of her own on the floor. "Since she died."

"Oh," Lena said, then continued after a quiet moment, "several of my family died during the initial riots the first year the crops failed, then a few others during the efforts to control the Wendigo outbreak. Most of them were military or police. They thought they were protecting people."

She pulled a card from the central deck, considered her hand, then laid down another. "After my father died, my husband and I decided to defect. We left the city and found a group of rebels to team up with. It was there that he was turned."

I found it... interesting, to learn about my companions' pasts. They had their own tragedies, terrible tragedies, but... they *were* still human. Despite losing everyone and everything they loved, they had the possibility of a future where they didn't have to constantly fight and kill for their own sanity and survival, where they could rebuild... something.

If I thought too much about it, I got uncomfortably close to being jealous. All I had left was my search for my brother's fate, and after that... I would still be a Wendigo. Nothing would change. I would still be a creature of hunger, a danger to everyone around me. I couldn't gain; only yearn, only hunger, only lose.

If I had been a completely rational being, I would never have set out on this trip. It wouldn't change anything, after all. As it was... perhaps I still did have some human yearnings, after all. I just wanted closure.

I sat, sliding down the wall until I completed a small triangle with the two women. "Alright, show me how to play."

The day passed uneventfully. Finally, as the light streaming through the open window faded away, we prepared to leave, stashing supplies and shouldering packs. Amica thought she knew where we were, based on the road name I had given her, but she wanted to see it for herself, just to be sure.

I led the way, the dogs pacing out to either side of our small line, slipping in and out of view like shadows. We didn't see anyone on the foot-paths as we made our way through the neighborhood, though we did see sign of people's passage during the day.

As we neared the larger street, we began to see an occasional person; usually someone dressed in raggedy clothes providing warmth only by virtue of the sheer number of layers.

We paused to discuss our plan before moving further. Around us, I could see several pairs of curious eyes peering at us, most people too wary to approach any closer than a street's-width away. No one was particularly alarmed, which seemed odd to me, but then, if the discussion the previous night was any indication, there hadn't been any Wendigos here for several years.

I felt like a tiger in a zoo.

Amica read the street sign, then looked up and down the street to orient herself. "If we go south, it'll lead us to another main road going east, and then after a couple miles we can turn onto High Street and go south to the university."

"How far away are we?" I asked.

"Several miles," she replied.

"Lena, what do you think?"

Lena nodded. "Yeah, that's probably our best route."

I frowned. It would take us quite some time to get down there, though probably no more than one night. It was a doable trek, so long as we didn't get waylaid by anything unexpected.

"Alright," I said. "We should get going then, before these people try and pet the tiger."

They both looked puzzled for a moment, then followed my gaze to the half a dozen or so people standing in the shadowed alcoves of nearby buildings, watching us curiously.

"Agreed," Amica said, starting off down the street.

She led the way, walking along the street itself where the snow had been cleared to only a thin, slick layer, broken up by glimpses of bare asphalt. It was faster-going than the inconsistent paths lining the street, though it did leave us visible to patrols, and the plowed snow-piles lining the street made it mildly difficult to leave the street in some places.

We only encountered two patrol groups before we hit High Street, though, and in both cases their headlights were visible from far enough away to give us sufficient warning to get out of sight.

High Street was even clearer than the previous streets. Nearly the entire street was black with visible asphalt, and there were even a few shoveled sidewalks. We started passing people here who didn't appear to be homeless, but simply out for a night-time stroll or errand. There even appeared to be a smattering of bars still operating, which were, while not teeming, each serving a fair number of patrons.

"I can't say I've seen this many people out at night in years," Amica commented.

"They would never be out this late in Wendigo territory," I agreed.

She nodded. "I guess your intel was right. There aren't Wendigos here."

"If they eradicated them here," Lena asked, "why didn't they do so in other cities?"

I shrugged, stepping around an uneven chunk of snow. "I always thought we were allowed to live to control the people. They aren't going to complain about food and energy shortages when they have a predator prowling the streets. It makes the Enforcers protectors rather than jailors."

"They don't seem too poorly off here," she commented.

I gave another shrug. I wasn't sure whether I agreed or disagreed with her sentiment. There certainly wasn't enough to
172

go around for the raggedly-dressed trio I had spoken to last night, and for others like them, but at the same time, these open bars and existing nightlife spoke of at least some affluence in the city.

I watched as a couple walked down the street across from us, my gaze lingering on them as they paused to turn and enter a bar. They seemed relaxed, one of them laughing at something the other said, but the laugh didn't last long. There was something about their manner that seemed almost forced, as the laugh was replaced by wide, pleasant smiles.

Well, it wasn't my business to unravel the social lives of the lucky. I turned and continued on with the others.

Patrols became more frequent as we neared the university area and the buildings became ever-increasingly occupied, housing originally built to house students now re-purposed to house those who had moved in from the outskirts of the city to seek safety in numbers. The university itself was no longer functioning as a university. Instead, much of it appeared to have been repurposed as training grounds for Ohio Enforcers.

Having been a researcher here herself, Amica would know her way around the campus better than any of the rest of us would, and she continued to take the lead. My familiarity with the area was based only on what I had been able to glean in my previous searches for my brother, and Lena hadn't lived near the main campus area.

Amica led us away from High Street before we hit the main campus area, moving from the well-cleared, fairly populated street to one less maintained. After a few blocks, the streetlamps, which had been maintained along High Street, were no longer shining, leaving us in the dark.

I paused once we were out of the last street-lamps' light, whistling over the dogs and taking the opportunity to let my eyes adjust back to the darkness as I took in the neighborhood. Amica quickly noticed that I wasn't following and stopped, looking back.

"Is something wrong?" she asked.

I shook my head. "Just checking the surroundings. How are we approaching the campus area?"

"We'll go down along the river," she replied, "and follow it nearly to where we need to be without having to go into the campus proper. The labs we want are near the hospital."

The hospital. What an unpleasant thought.

"Alright," I said. "Lead the way."

There was a walking trail near the river. We tried to follow it, but after a short time found that it was heavily frequented, mostly by people who looked like they wanted to avoid the Enforcers nearly as much as us. Still, as unlikely as it was that they would turn us in, it would be best to avoid too many witnesses to our passage, and Amica led us down the bank to the shore of the river itself.

The surface of the river was frozen, being more broad than it was swift, though I wouldn't have trusted the ice at its center to hold. Thankfully, we didn't have to cross it, just follow it, and after several more minutes, Amica led us back up the embankment.

We paused, looking out toward the research buildings. I recognized them now, from back when Ryan first joined the research program. I hadn't been able to get close back then; the area had been too heavily patrolled. Originally, those
174

buildings had housed various biological focuses, including a rather prominent cancer research department, but many scientists had been commandeered and reassigned for government-sponsored research after the world went cold, and again when the Wendigos appeared. Once the University had closed, there wasn't any support for the remaining general researchers, and many of them had moved away to seek funding elsewhere.

There were some researchers, though, who stayed. They had been offered contracts under the military forces that came in to enact martial law within the city and control the riots and lootings, and the Wendigos.

"I was in that building," Amica said, pointing toward the building in question. It was in rough shape. In one section, many of the windows making up the entire side of the building had been blown out, and in the light from brightly-lit training fields across the street I could see a gaping, scorched hole about halfway up the building. I had never been able to find out for certain which building the Wendigo research had been conducted in, but I did know that that particular building hadn't been in that state the last time I was here.

"Are you sure what you're looking for will still be there?" Lena asked

Amica shrugged. "I hope so. The Wendigo research *was* in that building; it was one of the best buildings for such research. I don't know if they went in and retrieved *everything* after the explosion, or just the most important stuff."

I looked away from the building, over to the nearby exercise fields. A few ordered groups of young men and women stood facing a drill sergeant, occasionally turning one way or another, or marching a certain distance before executing a turn to march another certain distance.

"We'll need to avoid being spotted by the recruits," I said. "It looks like no one's using the building anymore, but that just makes it less likely that anything actually useful will still be there." I tried not to let my disappointment creep into my voice.

"We were using paper records at the time," Amica said, also looking out toward the practice field. "Computer networks weren't reliable enough, since power kept going out. We had to stop using the building after the explosion, so they might not have had been able to get to all of the records safely."

"What caused the explosion?" Lena asked

"We... weren't told," Amica replied. "Some of us weren't happy with that, but there *were* confidential experiments taking place in the building, and we knew that. No one knew *all* of the experiments taking place."

I frowned, considering our options, then glanced again toward the Enforcer recruits, who were executing some kind of complex turning maneuver. Without waiting for any further input from the others, I turned and started across the street to the scorched science building.

If we didn't find what we were looking for here, I had no more leads. I couldn't just walk into a military office and say "hey, do you know what happened to my brother?" As long as this shot was, I needed to follow it through.

Behind me, I could hear the others following, boots crunching on the snow. The Enforcers across the street were occupied enough with their maneuvers not to notice us, and we slipped by undetected in the darkness. The floor-to-ceiling windows on the ground floor were still intact. Several were

176

cracked, traced with spider-web patterns, but no large holes could be found in this part of the building.

I approached a door, tried it, and found it locked. It seemed a bit odd that a locked building, apparently unguarded and uninhabited, wouldn't have had all of its windows shattered by looters. Behind me, Lena started to voice the same unease, but I shook my head. "It doesn't matter. I'm going forward."

I picked up a nearby stone and shattered the glass of the door, the shards raining down in an excess of sound. We all stood motionless for several moments, listening for any sign that we had been heard, but all we could hear was the drill instructor, still barking out orders.

Turning back to the door, I reached my hand through, enabled the mechanism, and pulled it open.

The others slipped in behind me. The dogs immediately began sniffing the new area, investigating the strange building. Inside, the space sounded large, though it was difficult even for me to see exactly how far the room went, with the only available light streaming through the windows from the training field across the street. Moving forward, I walked into a wide desk, likely once used by a security guard or receptionist, and beyond that, recessed from the main area, was where Amica said the doors leading deeper into the building would be.

She led the way to those doors. As I followed, the dogs came up beside me, growling quietly. Amica paused.

"Jason?" she asked. "What are they growling at?"

"I don't know." I cocked my head, listening closely for any sound that suggested danger. After a moment of relative silence, broken only by the dogs' low growls, I heard something coming from the other side of the door. Footsteps?

"There may be someone in there," I said.

"May be?"

"I can't tell for certain. It's muffled by the door. It could just be particularly noisy rats." I sincerely doubted it was rats, but I wasn't going to let footsteps keep me from going forward.

"Rats?" Amica sounded unamused.

"I hate rats," Lena muttered behind me.

"Better rats than anything else," I replied. I took a breath and stepped around Amica. "I'm going forward, whether someone is in there or not. If there *are* rats, the dogs will scare them away."

I reached forward, finding one of the door-handles. To my surprise, the door was unlocked and opened easily.

"Huh," Amica commented under her breath as we stepped through. "That door was always locked. Still think it's rats?"

The dogs continued to growl as we continued into the hall beyond, but nothing jumped out at us. I stopped to listen, the two humans stopping as well to wait for me to assess our surroundings. This time, I heard nothing.

"We'll have to take the stairs," Amica said. I could hear her feeling along the wall, Lena slipping by me to keep one hand touching Amica for guidance as they moved. Though it was also a little too dark for me to see, I simply followed by sound, with the dogs trying to keep constant contact with me, brushing against my legs as they continued quietly growling.

Ahead of me now, I heard another door open as Amica found the stairwell. I followed behind her and Lena, making sure the dogs got through as well.

As the door thudded closed behind us, I heard another thud, quieter, above us. Another door closing? Definitely not rats.

"Don't stray far from each other," I said quietly. "What floor was the Wendigo research on?"

"Third," Amica whispered.

"I have some matches I could light," Lena whispered, "but I don't want to give away our location."

"Keep them handy, but don't light them yet," I agreed. "No need to broadcast our exact location to what, or who, ever that is.

We started up the stairs in the dark, each keeping one hand on the wall beside us, circling carefully upward. I brought up the rear, ears peeled for any untoward sounds.

I didn't hear anything until we reached the third floor landing, by which time I was as tense as the dogs, ready for something to come out of the darkness at us without warning. As we reached the landing, though, I heard yet another door shut, this time below us, followed by the distinct sound of bipedal footsteps coming up the stairs. I turned to face the approaching footsteps, teeth bared in the darkness, while behind me, Amica pulled the door open and went through with Lena. I followed, walking backward and feeling behind me for the doorway, not wanting to turn my back on whomever was approaching until I had the dubious safety of a door between us.

Chapter 15

A bright light switched on as I closed the door, blinding me after prolonged exposure to darkness.

I turned, squinting painfully in the bright beam of the flashlight, trying to make out the visage of whoever was behind it.

"Who are you?" a male voice snapped from behind the searing light. Behind me, the door opened again, and another person stepped through, doubtless the one we had heard coming up the stairs.

I didn't reply, tensing and preparing to fight as we were flanked. I couldn't turn to face the person behind me; that would leave the man with the flashlight to do what he wished. At the same time, I really wanted at least some knowledge of what kind of person was behind us. I snarled wordlessly at the trap I was in.

Amica was the first to speak. "That depends on who you are," she replied, one hand lifted to block some of the light. Beside her, Lena risked a glance behind us, then tried to sidle closer to me.

The man with the flashlight liked neither Amica's response, nor Lena's movement. He raised the large mag-light as if to strike. "I'm not going to ask again. Who are you, and why are you here?"

A hulking, mountain of a person stepped from behind us into the periphery of my vision, cutting off Lena's movement by placing one hand firmly on either of her arms.

She didn't struggle, but she did look at me and speak. "Jason, they're Wendigos."

That was unexpected. Everything we had seen in the city so far indicated that Wendigos had been eradicated here. No one feared me, no one seemed concerned with hiding at night. Even the homeless, the weak and easy prey, said that there was nothing to fear but the Enforcers.

Except... that one kid *had* said something about Wendigos being kept here under Government control.

If these were Wendigos, they may be willing to show us any remaining files hidden away in this building. We had encroached on what was obviously their territory, one they had kept very well hidden for who knows how long, and they probably just wanted to make sure we didn't mess up what they had going.

"We're looking for some old research files," I answered. My eyes were finally adjusting to the light, but I still couldn't clearly see the person behind the flashlight.

Amica glanced over at me, but didn't refute what I said. Lena, having gotten her message across, stayed where she was, wisely not trying to struggle out of the grip of the behemoth who held her.

The flashlight lowered, and enough light reflected off the floor that I could get a rough idea of the man who stood before me. He was taller than I was, and somehow even skinnier. His skin clung tightly to his bones, and he wore no shirt, exposing prominent ribs. His hair was light and long, hanging somewhat scraggly around his head. "What files are you here for?" he asked, tone less aggressive, though wary.

"We're looking for a study on family members of Wendigos. Specifically, on those who were immune."

He leaned down a bit, bringing his face close to mine as he met my gaze. After a moment of tense silence, he spoke.

"We don't have the files. They were taken."

That was disappointing.

"Do you know where they were taken?" I asked.

He straightened, and I relaxed slightly. After considering me warily for another long moment, he turned and walked away down the hallway, flashlight shining before him. "Follow me."

The muscle-bound Wendigo released Lena and pushed her slightly to urge her forward, and the five of us moved forward with him following behind. Ash and Shadow kept close beside me, their bodies brushing against my legs as we slowly made our way through the not-so-abandoned hall.

At the end of the hall we came to another stairwell. The tall Wendigo led us into it and up, climbing the stairs to the fifth floor. There, he led the way back into the building proper, where I could see why he took us up through a different stairwell.

Nearly a third of the floor was blown away.

The light from the practice fields across the street streamed in through the shattered windows and open wall. Bits of shattered glass and drywall still littered the floor. Below and above us, I could see through to the adjacent floors, and across the hole, a large mound of rubble blocked the other stairwell.

The tall Wendigo didn't stop to gawk at the destruction, however, but turned and led us toward the interior of the building, down an increasingly-intact hallway to a series of old offices. One of them had light shining from under the door.

He raised the hand holding the flashlight and rapped on the door. "You have visitors."

After a moment, the door cracked open, though I couldn't make out from this angle who was inside.

"Who?" someone asked from within. The voice sounded somewhat familiar, and yet… twisted.

I frowned. Familiar? Did I know this Wendigo?

"Some rogue, a couple humans, and a couple dogs. Looking for the Wendigo research."

"A rogue? This far into the city? What are they doing here?"

"Looking for the research, apparently." The tall Wendigo repeated drily.

There was a long pause before the person on the other side answered. "Fine. I'll take care of them."

The tall Wendigo nodded and turned away from the door, stalking past us back up the hallway. The other one remained where he was, and in the passing light from the flashlight I finally got a good look at him. He had the build of a professional wrestler - big, muscular despite the general atrophy that plagued a Wendigo's physique, and with a large mustache that almost seemed plastered on his face. He eyed us with a keen intelligence, though, and I quickly came to the conclusion that I would rather not fight him. I turned back to the door, which was still cracked open, and stepped forward through it.

The full brightness of this room was striking after the darkness outside, even with the recent light from the flashlight to mediate it. I shielded my eyes for a moment as I walked in, though I could hear the others entering with me.

"Shut the door behind you," the strangely-familiar voice said.

Someone, probably Lena, closed the door. I lowered my hand as it snicked shut.

The room was mostly furnished like an office. It had a desk, some chairs, and a couple gas lamps, which lit it fairly effectively. The small bed in one corner distinguished it from a normal office, though, as did the black paint over the window.

There was a Wendigo waiting for us. He sat at the desk, writing something down, not yet looking up at us. I couldn't see anything of his face, just a tousled mess of brown hair, but that was enough to trigger memory. My stomach dropped.

"Now," he said, "who the Hell do you..." He looked up, and as he and I met gazes, he fell silent.

"Jason?" he asked.

I didn't reply. All that I could do was stare at the person before me. Beside me, I was vaguely aware of Amica and Lena's confusion, though Amica figured it out first.

"We aren't going to need those files, are we?" she asked.

I shook my head, walking up to the desk. My brother, whom I had last known to be human, to be *immune* to the Wendigo curse, was sitting before me...

I looked him over closely, as he did the same to me. It was years since we had last seen each other, and I was fairly sure neither of us thought we would see each other again. Honestly, I had been nearly certain he was dead. "How?" I asked. "I thought..."

He flexed his hand, the one with the roughly-healed scar from a wound that I had inflicted. I *knew* he was immune. I had been the one to attack him.

"You would be surprised what a few years of government research can come up with," he replied, giving me a slight, tired smile. "But how did *you* end up here? And with two humans, even. That can't be safe."

"We did have another traveling companion that Jason's nearly eaten multiple times," Amica chimed in, leaning against the wall with her arms crossed. "He stayed behind at our last stop. I'm sticking with Jason because he's going to help me with some revenge in return for me getting him here."

"I'm just along because my settlement was burned to the ground and I didn't want to stay in a village," Lena said. Ryan stared at her for a moment.

"You're awfully nonchalant about traveling with a Wendigo," he finally said.

I chuckled as he echoed my own thoughts about Lena, and he turned his attention back to me.

"We have a lot to catch up on, Jason," he said, "and I *am* happy to see you alive and well." He sighed ruefully. "Unfortunately, there are some... factors to consider with this reunion. I have contracts I need to keep."

"Contracts?" I frowned, sitting on the edge of his desk. "Who the Hell would enter a Wendigo into a contract?"

Behind me, Amica coughed pointedly.

"That's not a contract, that's an agreement," I stated.

"I'll get to that," Ryan said. He smiled, though it seemed forced. "Again, I *am* glad to see you, Jason. I thought you would be dead by now."

I frowned. "Are you stalling for something?"

He shrugged. "Not really. There isn't anyone who comes around at this hour anyway, so what happens to you three is up to my own discretion. We're not waiting for anything but dawn." His expression turned more serious as he eyed me closely. "I would rather this go as well as possible."

"Why wouldn't it?" I asked him, leaning a little closer. I was worried. Now that I had found my brother, alive against all odds, I didn't want some shady government strings-attached deal to ruin it. "What do you have going on here?"

Ryan leaned back in his chair. "A lot." For a moment, I thought he wasn't going to continue, but as I was about to ask another question, he spoke again. "After you nearly ate me, which by the way, I hold no hard feelings over. I know now how the hunger gnaws." He paused before continuing. "After you nearly ate me but I didn't turn, I decided to enroll in one of the government-funded studies on the Wendigo virus. It usually passes from contact of bodily fluids: blood to blood, saliva to blood, even... other fluids. At that time, it was still active, and I wanted to see if I could help find a vaccine for it, or even a cure."

"Jason almost ate you?" Lena broke in.

"It was only a nibble," Ryan said, holding up his scarred hand. "He didn't mean it."

"I meant it, and you know it," I replied.

He shook his head. "You may have done it on purpose, but that doesn't mean you meant it. Given the choice, you wouldn't have, and I shouldn't have tried talking you down when you were that far gone."

Ryan looked from me over to Lena. "Has my brother told you anything about his past?"

"Not much."

"He told me some of it," Amica said. "He said his family turned him out; that his, your, parents would have nothing to do with him, and that they said he was a monster and already dead to them."

Ryan shrugged. "Yeah, that's pretty accurate."

"He also said that you didn't turn him away."

My brother smiled slightly. "No, I didn't. There wasn't a lot known about the condition back then. Most people thought that it only drove people who already had violent tendencies out of control, and that it could be controlled with enough willpower. Of course, there is some truth to that, but not a lot. It was more hopeful thinking than anything, really. But Jason and I thought that we could get it under control, so I brought him to my place to stay."

"It ended with me tearing the door down while he was gone," I broke in, "killing the couple down the hall, and then biting through his hand when he got back and tried to talk me down before I finished eating."

Ryan looked at me, then back to Lena and Amica. "I honestly wouldn't have minded turning into a Wendigo. We could have teamed up. But I didn't turn, and Jason ran away when I fell asleep. I hadn't heard from him since, until now." He finally turned to regard me again. "So, how did you track me down?"

"I kept an eye on you for a while after I left," I replied. "I... followed you when you moved, trying to gather information on the study you entered. When you stopped going home, I did a little more digging, but any word of the study vanished, and you with it."

He nodded, as if my story were simply corroborating his own experience. "I honestly had no idea you were keeping track of me," he said after a moment. "But the study did pack up and leave shortly after I entered it. It was more or less a front for another program. They tested anyone who entered to make sure they truly were immune, then they tested a bunch of psychological traits, though I'm still not sure what they were looking for. Anyone who passed muster was roped into the program, closed off from the outside world, and shipped to a secret facility."

I frowned and was about to speak, but Amica beat me to it.

"If this facility and project were so secret, why are you telling us about it?" she asked.

"Because Jason is my brother, and because none of you, except maybe the dogs, are supposed to be allowed to leave to tell anyone about it. Simply confirming the presence of Wendigos in the city is punishable by death, so since you're in for an inch, you may as well go in for a mile."

"That's not very reassuring," Lena said.

He looked at her, then back to me. "It's not supposed to be," he said. "I have a plan, but for now, you need to know what you've gotten into."

"Alright," I said, gesturing for him to continue. "Keep going."

Chapter 16

"They didn't tell us what the purpose of their actual experiment was at first," Ryan continued. "I just thought they wanted to quarantine us, maybe to make sure our blood wasn't contaminated or something. I don't know. In any case, they took several samples a week, but other than that, I didn't have much to do at first. They provided for me while I was there, but I didn't actively participate in anything for a month or so."

He paused, brows furrowing slightly. I recognized the look. Something about those memories was bothering him.

"What did they have you do?" I asked.

Ryan smiled slightly, his expression deliberately clearing. "Instead of taking samples, they injected them. Apparently by this time basic research ethics had been discarded, because I wasn't even given a permission form to sign. They just assured me that it was part of finding the cure for the Wendigos, and I went along with it."

He took a deep breath, apparently gathering his thoughts. "Most of the injections didn't do anything, to me at least. They always injected two or more of us together, and usually at least one person had a terrible reaction, usually rashes, swelling, or fevers. There were a few injections that caused such reactions in me, and I was given a few days to let it wear off each time before being put in the next injection group. After a couple months..."

Another pause, this one longer. "There were stronger reactions. Some people dropped completely, frothing at the mouth or simply collapsing unconscious. A few never woke up. I wasn't present the first time an injection successfully caused a transformation. I was in the second group to be injected with that batch, though, and, well…" he gestured at himself.

"They developed a version of the virus that overcame immunity?" Amica asked.

He nodded and sat up, leaning forward across the desk. "And they changed the virus further. They made us different than the original Wendigos, like Jason. They made us…" he frowned, searching for the right word, "tame. They made Wendigos who could be conditioned and trained with the promise of meat, who are compelled to eat, but get no satisfaction from getting it themselves."

I frowned, confused and disturbed by what he was saying. "What do you mean?"

"We can't stomach normal human flesh," he replied. "It needs to be treated, supplemented with something that only the government handlers know, so even though we kill, we can't eat. And yet, we have the same hunger and *must* eat, which compels us to kill what and who they tell us to, for the promise of any sort of satiation, held over us like a carrot on a stick."

"The hunger without the means to appease it," I echoed quietly, my frown deepening. "They turned you into weapons."

He nodded, leaning back again in his chair. "This entire city is an exercise in control," he explained. "Anyone who steps out of line, talks about what they shouldn't, or goes where they shouldn't, disappears. So, we officially don't exist, but we're always present in the shadows, watching and keeping order,

190

fueling the government's greed for control. The closer you get to downtown, the stricter the control."

That explained the strange undercurrent of forced ease I had picked up from the night-time shoppers on the way here. They were all living under a facade, all carefully sticking to approved actions and expressions, in fear of what lurked in the shadows. And that explained why no one had been terribly afraid of me, either. I wasn't in the shadows. I was there, in front of them, and thus, didn't register as a threat.

"That's terrible," Lena said, frowning. "You're completely dependent on them... that makes you little more than slaves."

Ryan chuckled. "We aren't human. Laws for humans don't apply to us, and thus, we aren't classified as slaves. At best, we fall under research ethics standards, but no one pays attention to those anymore."

He shrugged and continued as Lena opened her mouth to argue his statement. "It's how they justify it, even if it's wrong. It's not like we have any choice in the matter or anyone to speak up for us. None of us know what they put in the food. We don't know whether we're missing something necessary for digestion, or if we need something that's not normally in human meat, and unless we know what it is and how to get it, we're bound to them like faithful hounds."

The whole situation was horrendous. Unethical government experiments... not so surprising, but still terrible. But my brother, alive but essentially enslaved...

"Do you know if they've tried this in any other cities?" Amica asked.

"I don't know," Ryan replied. "As far as I know, this was the primary city for the initial experiment. They may have implemented it elsewhere, but I haven't gotten much information about the rest of the world over the past few years."

I looked around the room. It was a normal office as far as I could tell, never having been used as a research laboratory. But many of the rooms we had passed on the way here were old laboratories, still containing most of their equipment.

"You're surrounded by old research equipment," I said. "Think you could use it to isolate whatever they're putting in the food?"

Ryan raised a brow. "None of *us* have the training for that, and I don't think you do either. Molecular stuff wasn't really your thing, was it?"

"No, not really..."

"And," Ryan continued, "we don't have electricity to power those machines. For now, we're stuck where we're at."

"For now?" I echoed.

He smiled. "Well, it is policy that any Wendigo found within the city must be turned in to the governmental authorities for integration into the program." Ryan leaned back in his chair, eying me. "Though I have always taken some liberty on how long I keep them around before turning them in."

He gestured toward Amica and Lena. "Certainly I don't have to report *them*. They can go wherever they want, even into military facilities, as long as they don't get caught."

I followed his gesture, eying the two humans and wondering what sort of plan he was thinking up.

"What do you want us to do?" Lena asked.

"I'm thinking we have two options. One, I turn Jason in, and while I'm doing that, you two slip in behind us and infiltrate the facility."

The difficulty there would be actually getting Amica and Lena inside without raising suspicion.

"And the other option?" I asked.

"We disguise them as Wendigos, I turn in all three of you, they bolt, we pretend to kill them, and then they wash off the disguise and infiltrate the facility."

Though the second plan addressed the issue of getting the humans inside, it seemed more complicated than practical.

"Both of those involve turning me in," I noted.

He nodded. "It's the only time we get into the facility. Until they can sedate a wild Wendigo, they have us guard them."

Amica spoke up. "Why don't you just attack them when you're bringing another Wendigo in? It would save you having to rely on us."

"And then what?" Ryan asked. "If we attacked the scientists in the facility, they would punish us by witholding food. There have been a couple of us, including the Wendigo who was in charge before me, who were driven permanently into hunger insanity."

I scowled. "So, what are you going to do this time? How will you keep them from altering me, and starving you?"

He sighed. "That's going to be the trick. We might just have to fight them this time, and hope that we can find files on what it is they feed us."

"I would rather not depend on that."

"It would be best not to do so," he agreed. He was silent for a moment, considering the options. "The thing is, our options are very limited. If we go in, this is going to be an all or nothing endeavor."

"Would you rather stay their servants?" Lena asked.

Ryan looked over at her, frowning. "That's the question, isn't it? An assured and sane existence in return for obedience, or eventual hunger insanity in return for freedom. If we don't find what it is they add, or if we can't get it ourselves once we do know, then that's it for us."

A knock came from the door. "What is it?" Ryan asked.

"You're wanted," someone said from the other side.

Ryan sighed and stood. "We'll decide tomorrow. For now, I'll have someone take you to a place where you can sleep. No one here will bother you two Normals. Jason, are you good?" he asked pointedly.

"My hunger's fine for now," I replied.

He nodded as he opened the door. Outside, the large, hulking Wendigo was waiting. "Alfie, take them to a guest room," Ryan said. "I'll head down to meet the goons. Do you know who wants me?"

Alfie shook his head.

"Alright, fine. Send Susan down to accompany me after you see these three to their room. They are our guests, treat them like it."

Alfie eyed Amica and Lena with suspicion, more or less ignoring me. Apparently Wendigos were more trustworthy than Normals around here.

Ryan turned away and headed down the hallway toward the stairs, leaving us with Alfie, who, after a few moments, gestured for us to follow him before also turning down the hallway.

We followed, and he led us up the stairs another two floors before leading us down another hallway, this one less exposed than the one on the fifth floor.

194

"How stable is this building?" Amica asked.

Alfie shrugged. "It's been standing since it was damaged, so it's stable enough," he replied. "Apparently it's a bit chilly, exposed and without electricity, but we don't really notice. I'll bring you Normals some blankets."

He left us in a room that used to be another office, though was now furniture-less. The carpet remained, as did a single window in the far wall. It was bare, but would suffice for sleeping.

Lena and Amica pulled their sleeping bags from their backpacks as Alfie left for some blankets. He returned a few minutes later with six of them, apparently not knowing how many the two humans would need and wanting to make sure there were enough.

Once he was gone, we all started settling down for the night. Amica and Lena each took a blanket, and we gave the remaining ones to the dogs, who curled up together happily. I would sleep next to them for the night, and wouldn't need any blankets of my own.

Amica kept looking at me like she expected me to say something, but I remained silent. I didn't feel like there was much to say. I found my brother. Against any of my expectations, he was alive. But... how much better was a life like his than death? Not only a Wendigo, but leashed to those who changed him and forced to rely on the handouts of his masters just to remain sane.

I lay down next to the dogs, my back to the others. Over on their side, Amica and Lena talked softly for a times, but I wasn't listening, lost in my own thoughts.

It wasn't part of our agreement to free my brother. I honestly hadn't even expected to find him alive. Amica had no bindings to anything to do with Ryan's plan, aside from keeping me alive long enough to fulfill my part of our agreement. Though, come to think of it, taking out the pack would be easier if we could recruit my brother and his Wendigos. If we could free them from their dependence, perhaps they would help us with that, and my brother could stay with me afterward. I would have some semblance of family again.

Of course, that was assuming we *could* bypass the dependence. For all any of us knew, it was some chemical that couldn't be found or created outside the government's laboratories.

I mulled over my thoughts for several hours, the quiet darkness wrapping around me comfortingly. By the time I realized my thoughts were circling back through the same thing over and over, I had come to one main conclusion: I needed to get my brother out of here.

Chapter 17

Sunlight streamed through the window the following morning. For a few moments, it was almost like summer, warm and bright, no snow to worry about. I lay half asleep for a long moment, my thoughts wandering back to when Ryan and I had been children. We had a decent childhood: plenty of food, games to play, supportive parents. Ryan was younger than me by about a year. Our parents had wanted their children to be close in age, so we could play together.

We had climbed a tall sycamore tree near a creek that ran behind our house, and were faced with climbing back down. The climb down was always harder than the climb up.

Ryan's foot slipped. For a moment, I saw him hanging by one hand from a branch, before he lost his grip and fell to the ground below. The sound of him crashing through the underbrush was accompanied by a strange cracking sound as his leg snapped.

I hurried down as quickly as I dared, jumping down the last few meters and twisting my own ankle in the process. I ignored it to go to Ryan, who was doing his best not to cry from the pain.

The broken bone was visible under Ryan's skin. I couldn't carry him on my own, and he couldn't walk, so I ran back home to get our parents, moving as quickly as I could on my twisted ankle.

One day and a lot of pain medication later, Ryan was in a cast and I had a splint on my severely sprained ankle. Running on it had damaged it further, but I had succeeded in getting help for my brother. My ankle ached for years afterward.

Until I became a Wendigo, of course. There was no lingering weakness in it after that.

I opened my eyes and sat up, disentangling myself from the two dogs draped over and around me. Shadow yawned and didn't wake, while Ash opened her eyes for a few moments to watch me before also deciding that sleep was more important.

Amica and Lena were still asleep, lying out of the direct sunlight. Carefully, I picked my way past them to the door, slipping out without waking them.

There were no guards outside our door, just the hallway and a slight chill breeze coming from the gaping hole in the side of the building.

I wandered through the floor, taking a look at the abandoned laboratories. A thick layer of dust covered plastic bottles filled with various chemicals, while broken glass crunched under my boots as I walked. It looked like many of the glass bottles had broken when the building was damaged. Thankfully, their contents had long since dried, leaving several patches of white crystalline residue which I took care not to touch.

Footsteps behind me caught my attention, and I turned to see Ryan approaching. "Quite a waste, isn't it," he commented.

I nodded. "This stuff wasn't cheap."

"We've been able to salvage a few useful things," he commented, stepping forward to stand beside me. "Unfortunately, none of us are trained chemists or biologists, so…" Ryan shrugged, "there's only so much use we can get from what remains."

We were both quiet for a few moments, looking over the destruction. "About that plan," I finally said, "what do you think the chances are of it actually succeeding?"

He didn't answer right away. When he did, his voice was tired and he refused to look at me. "It… doesn't look good. If we can't find a way to supplement on our own whatever it is we're missing, then we're as good as dead, and that's assuming we get out of there alive in the first place. There is a very good chance this is all just a suicide mission."

"And if you can supplement? What will you do then?"

Ryan frowned. "I honestly haven't thought much of that. We'll probably leave the city, or at least, I will."

"You're welcome to come back with me," I said. "Although…" I frowned, "you know, I wonder… There's a pack of Wendigos in Chicago that's been allowed to operate unchecked. It's not normal for Wendigos to pack up like that. The government never allows it, but they've allowed that group to remain."

"You think they're like us here?" Ryan asked.

"Maybe," I replied. "Or maybe they're part of a different experiment. At least one of them I already knew. We weren't *friends*, exactly, but I know she turned during the initial infection wave. If the government's done something to her, it would have been after that."

"They *can* modify Wendigos," Ryan commented. "It doesn't require starting with a human."

I nodded.

Ryan turned back to the window, looking out over the city pensively. "Your human companions should go get breakfast. They can go out into the city with no problem. I'll supply some money for them."

"Thanks. I'll let them know. Anything they should look out for?"

"Nah, they should be fine. Our lack of existence is enough to keep most people happy enough, and rumors that we *do* exist keep the unhappy ones in line, so the city's pretty calm."

He turned and walked back to the door, his boots crunching on broken glass. I followed, and we went back to the room where Amica, Lena, and my dogs waited. They were awake now, the dogs whining to be let out to go to the bathroom.

"You two can go out into the city for food," I said. "It should be safe. Can you take the dogs with you?"

They nodded and, after being given some money for food, left, leaving me alone with Ryan.

"I have some business to attend to," Ryan said after they were gone. "I would bring you along, but you shouldn't be seen with me yet. Feel free to go anywhere in the building, but be careful in the unstable sections." He paused, then added quietly, "I *am* glad to see you again, brother." He turned and left, leaving me to wander the building alone.

I was on the roof when I spotted the visitors. They appeared to be Enforcers, but from up there I couldn't be certain. They strode up to the building and inside, out of my sight.

Something about their timing bothered me. It was less than an hour after Amica and Lena left, and they hadn't returned yet. And here were these government cronies, paying

200

a visit to their pet Wendigos first thing in the morning. I stepped away from the edge of the roof.

It may be best to stay up here, out of the way, until whatever was going on was concluded. For all I knew, it could simply be a routine inspection, or visit, or whatever. But they could also be here for me, and if they were, I didn't want to be stuck out here on this open plateau.

Inside it was.

I slipped from the brightness of the mostly-sunny morning into the darkness of the stairwell leading back down into the building. A stairwell wasn't where I wanted to be either. I needed to be somewhere where I could easily move elsewhere if I needed to, if those Enforcers, assuming they *were* Enforcers, were here for me. Giving my eyes the moment they needed to adjust, I started quietly down the stairs, going down to the highest floor that I could remember having significant damage to the outside wall, offering access to the floors below it. If I had to, I could climb down to the lower floors, giving me a means of escape.

Crouching in the main hallway, I set myself to wait and listen.

I didn't hear anything for several long minutes. Even with several of the floors open to the outside and each other, voices didn't travel far between them. Finally, I heard the sound of boots on the stairs. Several pairs, and heavy. Not Wendigo.

I moved into one of the side rooms, one with access to the hole in the side of the building. Situating myself to the side of the door where I couldn't be seen by anyone out in the hall, I waited and listened.

"...wouldn't lie to you," I could hear Ryan speaking. "I don't know where he ended up. We were accommodating his human companions before bringing him in, that's all."

Someone else spoke, a gruff, angry voice. "Your orders are to *immediately* bring in *any* wild Wendigo that enters the city," he said. "You know that 01."

"I do," Ryan replied. "I apologize. Next time I will not be so accommodating to tired strangers."

"If he's gotten away somehow," the gruff voice said, ignoring Ryan's comment, "it's going to be on your head 01. *I'm* not answering to the boss on this one."

"I'm sure he's still around," Ryan assured him.

I wasn't happy with how that conversation was going. As the two were speaking, I could hear other people walking down the hallway, opening doors as they went and, by the sound of it, searching through each lab in turn.

The plan was going to kick in sooner rather than later, it seemed, and without the preparations we had hoped to be able to make. Although... I looked toward the outside wall, fresh air blowing in through the gaping hole. I could escape. Slip down to a lower floor... But that would be leaving my brother behind to face the consequences of my escape, and I couldn't do that to him.

Sighing, I took a few steps further into the room and leaned against the wall nonchalantly where I would be easily visible from the doorway. There was no way I was going to let Ryan take a fall for my sake. When the soldier shoved the door in, I eyed him casually. "Looking for me?" I asked.

He seemed surprised at first, but quickly recovered and leveled his gun at me. "Don't move. We're going to bring you in for registration and processing. If you cooperate, you will not be harmed."

I shrugged.

He turned and spoke to the people outside in the hallway. "I found him."

"Get him out here," the gruff voice said.

The soldier stepped into the room and to the side of the doorway, keeping the gun pointing at me. He gestured toward the door and I obliged him. He followed me out, no doubt still keeping his gun on me, and closed the door behind him. How polite.

Ryan and a uniformed human waited for me in the hall. Soldiers were standing in doorways along the rest of the hallway, but I didn't pay them any attention. The Normal, who I assumed was the source of the gruff voice, looked entirely unpleasant. He had a ruddy complexion, with a face currently blotched red by irritation. His well-pressed uniform, not being the standard body armor and helmet of the common Enforcers, designated him as some sort of officer, more used to giving commands than to executing them. His medium-brown hair was cropped short, though he sported a bushy mustache, and he stood nearly as tall as us Wendigos, though with a large, tank-like build.

"Sir," Ryan said, "this is Jason. He is the Wendigo who arrived the other day, and who we were going to bring to you today before you barged in here to find him yourself."

"Watch your tongue, 01," Sir said, then addressed me. "Where're you from, monster?"

I glanced at Ryan, who didn't meet my eye.

"Chicago," I said.

"Get pushed out of your hunting grounds?"

"No. I just like going for walks."

Sir's eyes narrowed, and he gestured to one of the soldiers. A sudden "pop" of sound, and pain shot from one knee up and down my leg. My leg collapsed beneath me, unable to support my weight. I managed to catch myself with my hands. Did they just shoot me? They just shot me!

I snarled up at him, hunger roaring up from the anger and pain. "What the hell was that for?"

"I don't like your tone. You'll learn pretty quickly not to mouth off, or next time we'll shatter your knee permanently."

Well, I didn't like *him*, but I held my tongue. This wasn't the time, surrounded by guns and soldiers willing to use them. Sir motioned again, and one of the soldiers moved to the side of my injured leg and yanked me up by the arm.

"You're coming in for registering and processing," Sir said, "and then, if you're of any use to us, you will be trained and then given lodging, food, and security in return for your cooperation." He turned and started back down the hallway. Ryan followed right behind him, and the soldiers and me behind them.

I was taken to a large truck waiting just outside of the building. A few flakes of snow were starting to fall, melting on the hood as they landed. The soldiers nearly had to lift me into the back before climbing up themselves. I sat heavily against the side of the truck-bed, injured leg out, blood gradually soaking into my pant leg. Ryan was directed to the front of the truck, to sit with Sir and another soldier.

"Do you guys really think it was smart to injure me and bring me in hungry?" I asked the soldiers as the truck rumbled to life.

They didn't respond. At least two of them had their guns trained on me at all times. I knew, as did they, that by the time I could cause any damage, I would already have several bullets through my head.

The truck drove down the snowy street, its sound muffled by the mountains of plowed snow on either side. There weren't many people out and about, and those that were pointedly ignored the truck. They lived a careful balance of willful ignorance here. As long as they pretended there weren't any Wendigos, then there weren't any, and I supposed the same might be true for the government soldiers that were driving through. So long as they weren't acknowledged, they didn't exist.

Funny how the desire to survive can make people so blind.

We rode for nearly an hour, the truck having to navigate the roads slowly as the snow fell more heavily and accumulated on top of what was already there. The soldiers around me blew into their hands to try and warm them, despite the gloves they wore. I was fine, except for the pain in my knee. The bleeding had stopped relatively quickly, but it would take a while for the wound to heal, especially since that was the same leg I had been shot in several days earlier.

As we rode, I leaned back, looking up at the sky and trying to ignore my rising hunger. I couldn't appease it here, not without facing certain death. When I did finally get a chance to sate it... would it only be under the government's terms?

My thoughts wandered from food to Lena and Amica, and I wondered if they were still out in the city, or if they had been collected as well. After all, Normal though they were, they had been willingly traveling with a Wendigo. I'm sure that raise some brows among the government trolls. Not to mention that Lena was, not long ago, part of what amounted to a terrorist cell in the eyes of the government.

It was prudent to assume they were being brought in as well, though whether they would be brought to the same location as me was up in the air.

We pulled up to a tall metal fence. Coils of barbed wire lined the top, the barbs visible only as clumps of snow, nearly harmless in appearance under their innocuous covering. The truck remained stopped long enough for a guard to identify it, then the gate opened up and we went through.

It was difficult to stand. My knee had stiffened during the ride, and though the searing pain had dulled, I could barely move it and it wouldn't support any weight. The soldiers again helped me down from the truck.

Ryan and Sir led the way as the soldiers clustered around me to bring me into the nearby building. It was a typical utilitarian space, with a brick facade and three stories of boring windows in boring rows. I was sure that there would be a sprawling basement complex as well, and likely tunnels leading to nearby administrative buildings. Such tunnels could be places to hide, if they weren't well-monitored and if I regained the ability to walk on my own before they made me dependent on whatever substance they forced on Ryan's group.

Unfortunately, that wasn't looking likely.

I needed to get a moment alone with Ryan to see if we had *any* options available to us other than either rolling over and accepting whatever they saw fit to do to me, or goading them into just shooting me dead.

God I was hungry.

I stumbled at the doorway, causing the soldier supporting me to stumble as well. Without thought, I had him pressed to the ground, my nails ripping through the outer fabric of his body-armor, attempting to get to the soft flesh it was covering. My stomach was a howling void and I *needed* to ease that desperate, gnawing hunger.

Hands gripped me and pulled me back, and the cold metal of a gun pressing against the base of my neck snapped me back to myself. It had been a reflex, an instinct driven by hunger, and thankfully, these soldiers were trained well enough not to simply shoot me outright.

I held my hands up and leaned away from the soldier who had stumbled. He paused for a moment before picking himself up, collecting his gun, and taking a position in the group outside my immediate reach.

Another soldier, this one significantly more burly than the last one, stepped up beside me and yanked me to my feet... er, foot.

There wasn't any more stumbling. They took me through the entrance lobby and deep into the building, through winding hallways that no-doubt had some sort of rational layout that I couldn't currently grasp.

By the time we stopped walking, my knee was around the size of a grapefruit. I think. I hadn't seen a grapefruit in years. In any case, my knee was an ugly mess, and I just wanted to dig the bullet out and tear into the soft, bleeding flesh of helpless prey, digging my teeth into their muscles, ripping out chunks of...

The butt of a gun whacked me in the back of the head. Not enough to knock me out, but enough to snap me out of another lapse. I had dug my teeth into the shoulder-plate of the soldier beside me, my nails sunk through to the skin through the relatively un-armored arms of his outfit. I could smell his blood, and nearly continued regardless of consequences.

After a long moment and several deep breaths I released him. I couldn't take down all of them. Not by myself. Maybe if Ryan… no, wait, Ryan wasn't here anymore. He and Sir were gone, having left the group at some point without my noticing, and I was left alone with the soldiers. They pushed me through a doorway into a small, windowless room. I fell to my hands and good knee, and by the time I spun around, the door had been closed and locked behind me, leaving me alone.

The first order of business was seeing to my knee, and I tore the leg off my pants to get a closer look. The swelling was nearly obscuring the entrance hole of the wound itself. Gritting my teeth, I poked at it a bit, feeling for the bullet I was pretty sure was still in there. Along with a few shards of bone and cartilage I finally managed to find it and, likely causing even more damage in the process, dug it out. I couldn't stand leaving bullets in, even when they probably should be.

I looked at the bullet. It was a small thing, just enough to cripple with a precision shot. Undoubtedly some of the soldiers had been equipped with these while others were toting more deadly calibers.

Tossing the bullet aside, I made strips from the torn-off part of my pant leg and tied a makeshift bandage around the wound. Hopefully, the swelling would go down now that the foreign object was gone, and eventually I would regain full use of the joint. Probably.

Unfortunately, without the pressing need to tend to the wound, my hunger rose up with the intensity of a blizzard. I needed fuel to heal, and to live. I wanted to continue living, and to do that, I needed to eat, to consume any human who crossed my path. As the minutes passed, my hunger grew, consuming rational thought.

I didn't feel the pain as I stood, though my leg still wouldn't take my weight. Ignoring the imbalance, I threw myself at the door, hitting it shoulder-first. I would force it open, no longer how many hits it took. I would sate my hunger.

Chapter 18

I didn't want to leave Jason alone with the local Wendigos, but he was probably safer there than anywhere else in the city. I would never admit it, but I did feel a bit safer when he was around, though his dogs were pretty good protection in their own right.

Lena realized something was wrong mere minutes after we left the building. We were all used to being vigilant, but hers was more actively honed than mine from years of living as an Independent. She was the one who noticed we were being tailed and whispered the news to me.

The dogs seemed to pick up on her apprehension, and after a few moments of anxiously looking around, likely searching for Jason, they seemed to decide that they would be better off on their own than with us and ran off.

Or maybe they were just running around to flank the follower. These dogs were pretty smart, aside from giving their undying loyalty to a Wendigo. I didn't think they were quite *that* smart, though.

I didn't stop walking, and neither did Lena. We were just going to get something to eat; there was no crime in that.

No one stopped us as we walked. It took a while to reach a populated area with open restaurants and shops, but in that time, though we were still aware of being followed, we weren't approached.

It wasn't until after we had chosen a restaurant and ordered food that I felt a hand upon my shoulder.

"Ladies, may I have a word?"

I had a brief urge to direct a kick at a choice place on the man behind me, and judging by the scowl on Lena's face, she had a similar thought. I restrained, though, and instead turned to see who it was that approached us.

The man was tall, though not Wendigo-tall. He had the build of someone who spent his spare time exercising, and was dressed in the black body-armor of the Enforcers. The tip of his nose looked like it had been hit by frostbite at some point, and his short-cut dark brown hair was starting to turn gray.

"What sort of word?" I asked.

"That's up to you two," he replied. "Why don't you grab your food and we'll find a quiet corner to talk in."

"And if we don't want to talk?" Lena asked sharply.

"I do suggest you sit down and talk to me," he said firmly. "You're in a dangerous spot, and it's not going to get better by trying to run away."

Lena looked like she was about to stab the guy, but I grabbed our food from the counter and handed Lena hers. I was all for stabbing, but drawing that sort of attention to ourselves wouldn't help any of us. "Sounds like we don't have much of a choice," I said. "Sure, we'll talk for a bit."

We couldn't afford to make a scene here. The fact that we hadn't been black-bagged on the street meant that something more complicated than just eliminating us or pumping us for information was going down. I wanted to hear what this guy had to say before doing something rash.

I slid into a booth seat, Lena sliding in beside me and placing her knife conspicuously on the table.

"What do you want from us?" I asked.

"Just a chat."

"A chat," I echoed, skeptical.

"Look," he said, "you two are treading some dangerous water. People like us, normal people, we're not safe around Wendigos. You know that, right?"

"Of course," I replied.

The man leaned forward. "Then why are you consorting with them?"

I eyed the man. "I'm not *consorting* with anyone."

"Look, I'm just trying to help," he said, folding his hands on the table in front of him. "We know both of you came into the city with a rogue Wendigo, and that you followed him willingly. What is it you get from your relationship with him?"

I leaned forward, mirroring his posture. "Whoever your people are, I don't have to tell you anything. It's not illegal to travel with a Wendigo."

He smiled, though something harsh lurked behind his expression. "Then why don't you tell me why you're traveling with a terrorist?"

My eyes flickered toward Lena, who was scowling beside me, watching the man with unconcealed contempt. The man's smile widened. "Illegal or not, you must admit you haven't been keeping the best company, miss. So, why don't you tell me why you've chosen these particular travel companions?"

I took a bite of my food before replying. "If you were traveling across dangerous territory, who would you choose to protect you?"

"Not someone who would eat me."

212

I considered that for a moment. He had a point. "Touché. I don't like Wendigos, but I made a deal with that one. I was doing him a favor, and he was going to do me one."

"What sort of favor?"

Before I could refuse to answer that question, Lena leaned forward and spoke. "Why do you want to know all of this?" she asked. "You don't have any proof either of us did anything wrong, or you wouldn't be sitting here questioning us. And if you wanted to get rid of us, we would already be dead. What do you want?"

The man looked between the two of us before leaning forward and lowering his voice. "I want to help you. They… we… the government, the soldiers, we're keeping the Wendigos here as slaves. Sure, they're monsters, but they're *sentient* monsters. I've spoken with them, spent time with them. They're intelligent, rational within their bounds. It's not right to keep people as slaves, even monstrous people. It's not their fault they are what they are, after all. Whatever purpose you're here for with that new one, he's stuck here now. He's going to be made dependent on us, and then used as a weapon."

I looked the man over. "What's your rank? You aren't just a common grunt."

"I oversee the Handlers. We make sure the Wendigos don't do much damage in the city. Not that that's usually a problem. They've been trained to stay within their tower unless needed."

"And what exactly do you propose we do to help them?"

He shrugged. "Honestly, I don't think anything can be done for the ones already here. They're in the system, like I am.

I can't just walk away from being a soldier, and they can't just walk away from being weapons."

"You say they're weapons," Lena broke in. "What do you mean by that?"

"I would think it's pretty obvious," he replied. "People are unhappy. There isn't enough food, there isn't enough heat, there isn't enough jobs. The country's infrastructure is crumbling under this ice age. If there's something around for the people to fear more than their everyday troubles, their troubles will seem less troublesome. And if the government controls the source of that fear, they control the people. It's all about the control."

A logical course, if twisted and generally evil.

"So if nothing can be done about the ones here, what do you want to help us with?" I asked.

"I want to get that new one out of here before they turn him," he replied. "We've been watching you all, and he was scheduled to be taken in this morning, so it's likely he's already been taken into the compound. I'll help you get him out of the city, and you three can leave and never come back."

"Have you done this before?" Lena asked.

The man nodded. "Twice. The first time was successful. The second... Well, he knew the danger and agreed with me that being shot to pieces was better than being a slave."

I couldn't argue with that. I looked over at Lena to gauge her opinion.

Lena nodded, though she still looked like the situation didn't agree with her. "Alright," she said, "how do you propose we get him out."

In the end, we just walked into the facility. The Handler overseer, Cameron, had gotten us access badges and proper

214

clothes and escorted us in himself. No one questioned his presence, and so no one questioned ours. Unfortunately, I had to leave my gun behind, but so far it seemed like I may not need it.

He walked us through the hallway to a stairwell, then down to the basement. Judging by the map on the wall, most of the facility was underground. I had little doubt that most restricted areas weren't even on the map, and that the facility was much larger than depicted.

We were led to a hall flanked by several doors. Halfway down the hall, Cameron turned into one of the offices and we followed him in.

It was a claustrophobic little space. A computer sat on a desk with a chair behind it. Stacks of paperwork cluttered both the desk and the bookshelf standing against the far wall. There weren't any extra chairs, and the room itself was barely larger than a closet.

Cameron closed the door behind us.

"I'm going to go take a look at the current state of things. No doubt they'll want me there, anyway, to help with the process. When I come back, I need you two to listen to my orders *exactly*. We may need to evac quickly, so be ready to run."

I wasn't happy with being left in this small box-room to wait, with no word of what was happening outside, but thus far, this was the best option available to us.

"Fine," I said.

Lena eyed Cameron suspiciously, then shrugged.

He nodded, turned, and left us alone in the room.

Neither of us spoke much at first, keeping our eyes on the door and our muscles tensed, ready to run, but as time passed and it was apparent Cameron wasn't returning immediately, we turned our attention elsewhere.

"What do you think's happening out there?" Lena asked.

"I don't know," I replied. 'Think we can trust Cameron?"

Lena shook her head. "Not as far as I can throw him."

"But far enough to get us in here?" I asked.

She nodded. "We wouldn't have gotten in here on our own, after all. So, if you don't think he's trustworthy, and I think he's going to turn us into a science experiment, why are we still in here?"

A good question. I looked at the door. "We can get out by backtracking out steps, but we don't know where they might have Jason. If we wander off in a random direction trying to find him, we're not going to be able to find our way out."

She considered that, then stepped over to Cameron's computer. "Don't you think it's odd that he goes by his first name?" she asked, as she moved the mouse and started clicking around a bit.

"No. Is it odd?"

"For military folk it is. Darn, his computer's password locked. Not surprising, really, but I had hoped that maybe I could pull up something useful." She started rifling through the papers on his desk. "Not that I'd know where to look for anything useful, anyway. I haven't touched a computer in years. So, are we moving out, or waiting for that guy to come back and see what happens from there?"

I frowned, considering the dilemma. Without an escort, it would take just one person being suspicious enough to ask a question to discover our infiltration. On the other hand, we

216

were sitting ducks where we were. But why bring us this far if Cameron was just going to turn us in? We needed more information.

"Let's see what we can find in his papers first," I said. "They may tell us something about his motives."

I walked over to join Lena and grabbed a few papers to look over. Most of them were general reports, nothing too surprising or important. A few of them were delivery notices, usually of "food," and sometimes of clothes or other things presumably asked for by the Wendigos.

Unfortunately, the Wendigos' food was apparently treated with something made in-house, as there were no orders of anything that might be the additives we were looking for.

"Look at this," Lena said after half an hour of fruitlessly looking through papers. She held up a report from one of the research teams, then spread it out flat on the desk so I could read it.

"It looks like a new experiment," I said, looking at the date. The report was less than a week old. On it were listed what appeared to be several test subjects, designated by numbers, each followed by a list of increasingly unpleasant-sounding body modifications and health problems. All but one resulted in death. "Do you think they could be developing a new strain of the Wendigo virus?" I asked. Most of the modifications sounded like they would fit the general Wendigo physique, but amplified to a grotesque degree. Was *this* what they intended for Jason?

"I don't know," she replied quietly. "Whatever it is, it's horrific."

A key scraped in the door's lock. Shuffling the report back among the other papers, Lena and I rushed to our bags, scooping them up in preparation for running.

Cameron slipped into the room and closed the door behind him. "No need to run yet," he said, noting our readiness. "I got you in for a close look at the current experiments. We'll be able to get in, get to your Wendigo, and get out."

This seemed too easy. "How did you do that?" I asked.

"I told them you're inspectors from DC's research division." He moved to his desk, opened a drawer, and took out a couple of leather-bound folders. "Here. No matter what you see, don't ask too many questions. Just pretend to take notes and look unimpressed."

We took the folders and before we could ask anything further he was leading us out of the small office and back out into the hallway. I met Lena's eyes for a moment, and though she looked troubled, she shrugged. We didn't have much choice but to follow.

We walked for several minutes, passing several soldiers as we went. No one paid us much mind, and Cameron didn't stop to give anyone a chance to think too long about us. We passed through three doors that opened only with key-card access, until we were in what appeared to be a concrete bunker, split into two sections by a glass partition. Two people sat at a desk on this side of the partition, facing it and taking notes.

Cameron ushered Lena and I into the room. As I stepped in, my stomach dropped, the sickening feeling deepening as I looked through the glass.

A large, lanky creature was in the room beyond, laying on the floor. It looked either asleep or tranquilized, though it was starting to move a bit as I walked in.

The door closed behind us.

I stepped up to the desk and looked through the glass. The creature pushed itself onto its hands and knees, tried to stand, and stumbled sideways into the wall, off-balance and groggy from whatever it had been tranquilized with.

It wasn't just a *creature*, it was a Wendigo. Only, it wasn't like any Wendigo I had ever seen. It... *she* stood nearly nine feet tall, and while she wasn't any more gaunt than any other Wendigo, her skin had an even more ashen cast and looked nearly like translucent leather. Her sunken, solid black eyes appeared too large for her head, and her hands ended in long claws more suited for ripping than for holding anything. Sprouting from her head stretched two growths of bone, curling and branching asymmetrically upward, the skin around their base bloodied where they grew out from her skull.

As she struggled to gain her balance, she let out an inhuman shriek, clawing at the single door within her room.

This was what that report had been describing.

"What do you think?" Cameron asked casually. "This is the result of our newest experiment. Unfortunately, it *is* necessary to start with a Wendigo, and she's nearly impossible to control even with food conditioning. We think she may be best utilized implanted with a self-destruction mechanism and used to clear locations before troops arrive, with decommission once her task is complete.

For a moment, my throat was too bound with anger to speak. He was talking about clearing out *people*. This Wendigo was a machine with only the purpose to kill. How many children would it kill? Daughters like my own. I grabbed my anger and shoved it down, into a hole where it could wait and be brought out later. I was supposed to be an inspector. This was an act. We were here for Jason. He… oh God, they were going to turn him into *this*.

"It is quite an accomplishment," I finally said. "It's a pity it's so difficult to control. I'll look into allotting funding for the self-destruction mechanism."

I glanced over to Lena, who was looking at the creature with pity instead of anger.

"You mentioned we would be observing the procedure on specimen two?" I asked, nudging Lena to pull her attention away from the Wendigo.

Cameron nodded and led us through a side door, into a wide hallway separated into two lanes by thick iron bars. He led us to the far end of the hallway and through a heavily-reinforced door into a single room beyond, which had another door opening to the other lane of the split hallway we just came through, as well as a door on the far side of the room from where we just entered.

The room contained several large cages, each easily large enough to hold a person, as well as a drain in the center of the floor and a hose curled on a hook on one wall. Shelves lined the wall above the hose, containing several glass bottles filled with liquids, pills, and powders. In one of the cages lay Jason, motionless, a bloodied bandage tied around one knee and his face and hands crusted with dried blood.

Cameron retrieved a bottle of clear liquid and a syringe from a shelf, filled the syringe, and moved to inject Jason with it.

220

"What are you doing?" I snapped.

He looked over at me. "Waking him up," he replied. "He was tranquilized for the scientists' safety."

Lena rested a hand on my arm, though to calm me or for support I wasn't sure. I still didn't trust Cameron's possible motives, but right now, he was our only option.

"Alright," I said, "let's get him out of here. How are we getting out of the compound?"

Cameron injected Jason then straightened and backed away. "The laboratories have their own supply channels, just in case they have to be closed off from the main convoy schedules. We'll take the elevator up and I'll put you three in a truck. We have a shipment going from here to Chicago today, and it'll take you all the way there."

"What are you going to do about the other one?" Lena asked.

Cameron raised a brow. "I can't do anything. She's a high-profile experiment. Something happens to her, and I'm dead. This one," he nodded toward Jason, "as far as anyone here knows, the feds claimed. As far as the feds know, he's in our pack. It's as much as I can do."

"Can't you at least kill her?" Lena asked quietly. "That's… a monstrous existence. You can't just let her suffer."

He scowled. "I get a chance, sure, but she's built to take out both armed people and normal Wendigos. A bullet or two's not going to stop her."

Jason stirred, trying to sit up and falling against the bars of the cage. Cameron turned and undid the lock. "Come-on, Wendigo. You're moving out."

Jason lunged forward, grabbing Cameron's leg and digging in his nails, snarling as he looked up. With the drying and crusted blood covering his face and mouth, the snarl was terrifying, and for a brief moment I thought of what he would look like if turned into a super-Wendigo like that other one.

"Jason, he's helping us," Lena said.

He looked around at the familiar voice, spotted us, and let Cameron go, relaxing slightly and blinking multiple times. "How'd ya get here?" he asked, slurring a bit as he struggled against the remnants of the tranquilizer. Clumsily, he pulled himself out of the cage and braced himself against the wall, not putting any weight on his bandaged leg. "How'd *I* get here? How're we getting out?"

"Come on," Cameron said by way of answer, turning and leading the way out the far door. Lena and I moved to support Jason and followed him.

"We'll explain later," I said. "Let's just get out of here first."

Chapter 19

The truck's bed was sheltered by army-green canvas. We helped Jason up first, and then Lena and I climbed in behind him. The truck bed was half-filled with boxes, ready to be delivered wherever it was they were needed.

"It'll be a couple of hours until the truck leaves," Cameron said as he closed the truck's tailgate. "I'll keep attention away from you until then. Just stay in here and stay quiet. The truck'll be joining a convoy on the way out of the base, and is on a direct route to Chicago. Just stay in there behind the boxes and out of sight."

"What about Ryan?" Jason asked, more coherent now as the effects of the tranquilizer faded. "Did you find out anything about what they did to him?"

I shook my head. "No. I don't think we'll be able to. We just need to get out of here. You found your brother, now let's go do my half of the deal."

Jason's eyes narrowed. In the shadows of the truck, they looked nearly solid black, like that other Wendigo's had been. "What aren't you telling me?" Jason asked. "Where are my dogs?"

"Keep the chatter down," Cameron said sharply. "The Wendigos here are on leashes. They can't survive out there on their own. Your brother's one of the locals?"

Jason scowled but didn't say anything.

"You take your brother out of this city, away from the government, and you'll be signing his death sentence," Cameron continued. He pointed a finger at Jason, emphasizing his words. "Just focus on getting yourself out of here before you're stuck in a situation you can't get out of." He turned without waiting for a reply and went back inside, leaving us alone.

For a moment, it looked like Jason was considering leaving the truck and setting out on his own. I knew he wouldn't get very far, considering his injured leg and the number of armed soldiers no doubt stationed around the compound, but I was sure that it didn't matter much to him right then.

"Your dogs are fine," Lena said in a hushed voice. "They ran off on their own before Cameron approached us."

Jason took a deep breath, turning away from the open back of the truck and looking at us. "Who is he?"

"A handler," I replied. "He said he keeps the Wendigos here from stepping too far out of line. He got us into the facility and showed us..." I paused, but only for a moment. As terrible as it was, Jason needed to know. "He showed us what they were going to do to you. They weren't going to make you dependent, they were going to make you a monster."

I could see Jason frowning in the darkness. "A monster?"

"They've developed a more powerful Wendigo," Lena verified. "A killing machine, with more hunger, more strength, and less reason, designed to be let loose and clear out anyone alive ahead of a clean-up crew."

Jason was silent for several minutes. I suspected he was weighing that revelation against the desire to go after his brother and dogs.

"If you try and leave this truck," I said, "I'm going to let them shoot you."

"I'm not leaving," Jason said slowly after a long minute of silence. He slumped a bit more against the side of a box before adding, "it wouldn't accomplish anything."

We lapsed into a tense silence. Neither I nor Lena seemed to know what to say to make the situation more palatable. Honestly, there wasn't much *to* say. He was running to save himself, and leaving his brother behind.

At least his brother was alive.

I couldn't say the same for my daughter.

But we were finally heading back home, and this time I would make sure that, come Hell or high water, the Pack paid for what they had done. And then... and then I was going to go after the government that triggered all this in the first place.

A few boring but tense hours later, I heard footsteps crunching through the snow outside. The three of us didn't move, barely daring to breathe as people passed by lest we were heard.

Finally, after an eternity of breathless stillness, the weight of the truck shifted as the driver and passenger climbed inside, and the engine rumbled to life.

Jason shifted uneasily as the truck began to move, as if he was once again contemplating jumping out and making a run for it. When he bent his injured knee, however, he was forced to abort the movement, growling in frustration.

"You're brother's going to be fine," Lena said. "He's stuck here, but he's alive. You can always come back later and try again."

Jason didn't reply, sitting in sullen silence. Lena and I didn't say anything further, either, and the three of us settled down to ride and wait.

An hour later, Lena woke me. In the shadows, I couldn't see her clearly, but her expression appeared worried.

"Amica, I don't think I should go to Chicago," she said.

I rubbed my face, trying to get feeling back into my uncomfortably cold nose. The truck jostled as it hit a bump. "Why?"

"I'm used to living away from the city. In there, I'm just going to be shuffled into the masses, a husk waiting to freeze or be beaten to death by the soldiers then left out to be eaten."

"Is that what you think of cities?" I asked. "You came to Columbus fine."

"That was a temporary trip, and my village was destroyed. Everyone I knew, except Andrew, either died or ran like we did." She was quiet for a moment, before adding softly, "I should go back and see if anyone is still there."

I considered that. I was glad Lena hadn't split off from us before now, but what was there, really, to keep her with us, aside from having nowhere else to go?

"You aren't going to be able to find them by wandering in the wilderness," I said after a moment's thought. "Why don't you come back with us long enough to catch the train back out. It goes right by your old settlement."

Lena was quiet for a moment, then reluctantly nodded. "I just feel like something's wrong," she said. "This is too easy. Why wasn't Jason being guarded?"

"Probably because I was unconscious," Jason commented from his side of the truck. I hadn't realized he was awake and listening. "Who would be crazy enough to break into a

226

government research facility and free a Wendigo? But..." He broke off, shaking his head with a grimace, "I do agree that it was too easy."

"Are you alright?" Lena asked.

Jason nodded. "Yeah. Just... a bit of a headache."

I frowned, concerned by that. Wendigos didn't get sick... Perhaps he was dehydrated? "Jason, how did they capture you?"

His answer didn't leave me any more comfortable with the situation. Shooting him certainly seemed overkill, especially if all he had been doing was mouthing off.

"You don't remember anything else after they put you in that room?" I asked.

He looked out the back of the truck, where white snow covering bare trees stretched on for miles. "Nothing."

I followed his gaze, watching the barren landscape pass by. "I wonder what they fed you while you were out if it," I mused. I didn't like the thoughts crossing my mind. Had they addicted him to something? Infected him with some new virus? "How are you feeling now, disregarding the headache?"

It took a moment for Jason to answer. He seemed unsettled by the implications of my musing.

"Sore," he said, "but in control."

I nodded, wishing I had my gun, just in case. Sure, I liked Jason well enough, but he was still a predator, and if my misgivings proved correct, it would be better to incapacitate him sooner than later.

"How long before you're on your feet again?" I asked.

"If I get something to eat, I'll be able to bend my knee tomorrow," he replied. "But it'll be at least a week before it's back in shape."

"A week," I repeated, closing my eyes as I leaned back against a box. A week until we could even think about going after the Pack. I tried not to be disappointed; we did still need to figure out a plan of action, after all.

"You kept your part of our deal, Amica," Jason said. "I'll keep mine."

We lapsed into silence as the truck rumbled on.

I woke again a couple of hours later. Lena was asleep, curled up between a couple of boxes, and it took me a moment to realize that Jason had nudged me awake and was watching me closely.

"What's up?" I asked quietly.

"Something's wrong with me," he replied.

I frowned. "What?"

"I don't know."

There was something in his tone that I hadn't heard from him before. Fear?

"Everything aches," he said. "I don't know what's causing it."

"How hungry *are* you?"

He paused to consider his answer. "Fairly, but I can control it for now."

"How's your knee?"

He bent it. "Better than it should be," he conceded. "It was nearly shattered."

The mother in me wanted to tell him that everything was fine, and that we had nothing to worry about, but I didn't think that was true and I didn't make a habit of lying. I nudged Lena awake.

"Wha?" she asked, sitting up.

"They did something," I said. "We need to stay awake."

"Do you think they turned him into…" She didn't seem to want to finish that sentence.

I looked over at Jason, who looked more troubled than annoyed about the way we were talking about him. It was uncharacteristic of him to be so nervous. He must really feel out of sorts…

The truck stopped briefly. I looked out of the back, eying the buildings outside. We were getting closer to the city.

The atmosphere in the back of the truck was tense as we continued on. Jason buried his head in his hands, making no sound but obviously uncomfortable. Lena and I both stayed alert, watching him worriedly.

He became restless as we reached the suburbs, twitching and occasionally shifting uncomfortably.

"How's the pain?" I asked quietly.

"Tolerable," he replied. He shook his head and shifted position again. "It feels like insects are crawling beneath my skin. Everything itches. My bones…" he held up his hands, which looked nearly deformed in the dim light, the fingers too long and the muscles visibly twitching beneath his skin, "they're not right."

I couldn't think of anything to say in reply to the fear in his voice.

The truck continued into the city rather than stopping at the outskirts. I wasn't sure where it was going, but we were going to have to get off at some point, even if we had to jump.

We needed to get off before Jason lost control, but I didn't want to just leave him, and the worry in Lena's gaze told me she felt the same.

I could nearly see his bones shifting, his skin stretching dry and taut over muscles that writhed and twitched as he gained height. He kept his head down, clutched in his hands as if trying to stave off a terrible headache. I could imagine the change in his eyes, the vast dark hunger reflected within immense pupils.

Blood ran between his fingers, coming from his head, and I recalled the overgrowth of bone that had formed horns or antlers on that other Wendigo.

"Keep talking to us, Jason," Lena said. "You'll be alright. We'll find a way to keep you yourself."

I couldn't bring myself to repeat that lie.

"I don't think you can," he replied quietly. His voice was shaky and hoarse. "When we stop, you should run and leave me behind. Whatever they did, it's…"

"We're not going to leave you," Lena replied firmly.

Jason laughed. It seemed to me that he was barely keeping himself together, barely holding off a panic which would only trigger a final loss of control.

We all knew that this time, once he lost his sense of self, he wouldn't be coming back, and none of us knew what to do.

The truck stopped and was shifted into park.

For a long moment, no one moved.

Snow crunched outside. Jason jerked up at the sound. As he moved, I could see that his eyes had turned black, and the skin on his head had split open, bloody and bony growths spiking through the torn flesh. His attention was on the outside, and I held my breath, hoping against all evidence that he could hold himself together.

230

As I followed his gaze, I noted that we weren't in a military complex, or anywhere else that would make sense to stop in. In fact, this area looked... familiar.

I bit my lip to stop myself from saying something. We were mere blocks from my daughter's old elementary school. The convoy had gone directly to the pack's territory.

Chapter 20

"Jason," I whispered. "Still with us?"

He turned to look at me, and I had to fight not to shrink away from those vast iris-less eyes. His face was contorted, whether in pain or an effort to control himself I wasn't sure. After a moment, he nodded, but didn't say anything.

I heard the windows of the truck roll down and two people began to speak: one female, one male.

"There's no delivery scheduled," the female voice said sharply. "What the hell are you doing here?"

"Special delivery," the male said. "From the higher ups. Bit of a last minute project they wanted to test."

The female snorted. "More drugs to try on us?"

"Not this time. Something bigger. Check the back of the truck."

I jumped as someone grabbed my wrist, and looked around to see Lana, her eyes wide. "Amica, this wasn't an escape," she whispered.

The realization of just how thoroughly we had been set-up washed over me like icy water. Jason... they were testing him... their experiment... against the pack.

We all turned to look as a shadow fell over the back of the truck. A Wendigo stood there, eying us critically. Her hair was pulled back into a tight ponytail, and a long scar ran down one side of her face.

"*This* is what they sent us? A couple of humans and a..." she frowned as she eyed Jason. "What are you?" she asked.

There was silence for a few brief seconds that lasted an eternity.

"You shot my dog," Jason finally said, locking his eyes with hers. His voice was rough, and his syllables were warped around lengthened teeth, making it difficult to understand him.

Lena was still gripping my wrist, sitting behind me. I didn't dare to move, wishing more than ever that I had my gun.

The female Wendigo stepped back, eyes widening in realization. "Jason? What the... what happened to you? What did they do to you?" She sounded genuinely distressed, but then, anyone would be when faced with what Jason had become.

He moved forward, forcibly pushing the tailgate down with a screech of warping metal. In the light, he looked even more frightening. Blood was drying on his head where the warped antlers had grown from his skull, and he stood nearly two feet taller than he had before. He looked nearly skeletal standing there, sickly gray skin stretched tight over bones and stringy muscles. His arms were obscenely long, and it almost looked like he would be more comfortable on four limbs than two, while long fingers and longer claws looked able to penetrate clear through someone.

He swayed for a moment, then took one step closer to the other Wendigo.

I heard several new voices shouting in alarm as Jason took another step forward, presumably the other Wendigos realizing that something was wrong.

To her credit, the pack's leader didn't back away as Jason approached. Instead, she straightened, one hand reaching for the gun at her hip.

"It was business, Jason. I was making a point. The dog didn't die, did it? Come on, Jason, what did they do to you?"

Jason leaned forward, resting his weight on his hands with his face scant inches from hers and said something that I had to strain to catch. "I know," he growled. I could see he was breathing heavily, and it seemed that every word was taking an effort to get out. "But I *want* to kill you. And them. I *will* kill... you all... " The muscles across his shoulders jerked as if he were barely holding himself back from lunging at her.

After a moment, he met her eyes again and said clearly, a pleading note clear in his voice, "shoot me."

"What?"

"Rachel," Jason snarled. "Kill. Me. Now."

"Jason, I can't just..."

He lunged.

Rachel pulled out her gun, but it was knocked out of her grasp as Jason hit her. They fell back to the ground, and Rachel used the momentum to kick Jason back and over her before rolling free. I could see other Wendigos running into the fray from all directions. Three, four, six of them, putting the odds at seven to one against Jason.

It didn't look good for the pack members. It seemed that nothing they did phased him at all. Biting, clawing, a few even got a shot or two off before Jason reached them and pulled off their arms. And the more he fought, the more frenzied he became.

"He's not coming back from this," Lena said quietly behind me.

234

I agreed with her, but didn't want to say it out loud. Jason was gone. Whatever the government had developed had turned him into nothing more than a weapon and had stripped him of any reason or humanity.

The truck was relatively safe, but I knew that once Jason was done killing the Wendigos out there, he would come after the fresh, human meat in here. In fact, as soon as they were sure of how well their little experiment turned out, the soldiers would probably drive out of here, either taking us with them in the back of the truck, or leaving us here, exposed and alone.

"We're not going to leave him like this," I said, making a decision. "Come on."

I hadn't come this far just to run away again. The pack was right here within my sights, their leader skirting around the fray as she looked for an opening. And even if my own revenge wasn't a factor, I had told Jason that I would take him out if he lost his mind.

I wasn't going to go back on my word.

We slipped out of the truck, crouching low to the ground and hoping the fight would occupy the others for at least a few minutes more. Rachel's gun lay discarded in the snow, and I retrieved it.

Lena followed behind me as I moved forward.

Rachel spotted us and moved around to intercept. I raised the gun, aiming at her, but she held her hands up in appeasement, eyes more on the fight than on us.

"What the hell happened to him?" she snapped, crouching down in the bloody, churned-up snow beside us.

I eyed her sharply. At this moment, we had a common enemy. Was that enough reason not to shoot her immediately?

"The government got to him," Lena said, sparing me my deliberations. "We don't know how they did it, but they have another one like him."

"Another one?" Rachel looked appropriately alarmed. "So it's not just a one-off venture, then," she added under her breath. "None of us are safe."

"We need to take him out," I said as the pained scream of one of the pack Wendigos cut through the air. Jason took a moment to pull their intestines out of their body before turning to deal with the Wendigo clawing at his back.

"Agreed," Rachel said. She looked down and spotted her gun in my hands. "I can take a hit or two. I'll distract him, you shoot him. Make sure it's a headshot."

I nodded. We wouldn't get a second try.

Heck, we might not get a first.

I held the gun ready, and Rachel ran forward. All of her Wendigos were either dead or in the process of dying, what was left of the snow turned red with blood and viscera. One of them wheezed out something that may have been a word and reached out to her as she darted past, but she paid him no mind and instead went straight toward Jason, who had turned his attention toward the trucks.

Jason's back and limbs were covered in gashes and bites, slowly oozing blood which was quickly clotting into black streaks.

The trucks rumbled into gear as the soldiers suddenly decided they had enough data.

The beast that had been Jason gathered himself to leap at the truck, but Rachel hit him first. She darted in, raking her own nails along his side as she passed, then changed direction, throwing up a spray of snow, and started back toward us.

He screamed in anger. The sound was chilling, more wildcat than human. I took a deep breath to steady myself, and readied the gun. Turning, he stalked after Rachel, who had stopped running and was facing him, keeping his attention as she walked backward toward us.

She miscalculated how fast and far he could jump.

The beast plowed into her, driving her to the ground with the sound of audibly cracking bones. He had his jaws on her shoulder, sharp teeth shredding skin and muscle from bone.

I had a clear shot, so long as those antlers couldn't stop bullets.

I took it.

They couldn't

Blood exploded into the air. The beast jerked back and collapsed.

As the ringing of the gunshot faded, the scene descended into eerie silence, barely broken by Rachel's pained wheezing from the ground. The soldiers had taken their opportunity to leave and were long gone.

I lowered the gun, taking a deep breath to try and stop my hands from shaking.

Lena walked forward first, and I followed her. She went up to Jason's body, but I stopped first at Rachel.

The Wendigo was lying on her back in the snow, one arm obviously broken. By the sound of her breathing, several ribs were broken as well. She looked up at me and tried to push herself up on her good arm.

I lifted the gun, and she stopped moving. Good, she wasn't too overcome by hunger yet to be rational.

"What are you doing?" she wheezed. "Just going to shoot me while I'm down? I helped you."

"You killed my daughter," I replied, and shot her.

"What did you do that for?" Lena asked once the sound of the gun faded away, leaving us in true silence. She had stood, apparently convinced that Jason was, in fact, dead, and now seemed determined not to look at his body again.

"Revenge," I replied simply. I felt numb. The leader of the pack was dead, and I had my justice. Or at least, something I could convince myself was justice. Jason was dead, which was... well, if I was honest with myself, it was terrible. He had been a decent guy, until the government got their hands on him.

The sound of an approaching truck broke the silence of the street. I looked up to watch it approaching, but didn't make any move to do anything.

Lena pulled the gun from my hand, apparently concluding that it would be better used in her hands at the moment. She leveled the gun at the driver as the truck approached, but lowered it as the truck drew close enough for us to see who was driving it.

The truck jerked into park before coming to a complete stop, and the driver jumped out, followed closely by two dogs, and ran up to us.

"Where is he?" Ryan demanded.

I pointed.

His shoulders slumped, but he didn't walk any closer to Jason's body. "I see. Good."

"Good?" Lena echoed, scowling. "What do you mean, 'Good'? That's your brother."

"That's why it's good that he's dead," Ryan snapped clenching his hands and snarling at her. After a moment, he took a deep breath and crossed his arms. "I managed to get into some records and found the data on their experiment. They needed a fresh specimen, a wild Wendigo, and Jason ended up being it. I didn't know that's what they planned."

"Oh," Lena said quietly. "I see."

"They wanted to do a field combat test," he spat, "so they sent him here to one of their other test packs, one more troublesome than mine." He kicked the ground in frustration. "He never stopped looking for me, and I just... handed him right over to those monsters."

I didn't say anything. What would have happened if Jason had gotten through the pack and gone on to rampage into the rest of the city? How many people could have been killed? Who really was the monster here? Government or Wendigo? I had to agree with Ryan.

He scowled and turned back toward the truck. "You two should get out of here," he said. "Things are going to get dicey once they make more like him. It looked like they're working on a new version of the original virus, too, so best to stay away from people for a while. Apparently they're making a move to consolidate and more tightly control the remaining population. Seems they just can't get enough power and control to satisfy their *own* hunger." He was quiet for a moment, then added, "take his dogs with you?"

"Do you not want to take them?" I asked.

"I'm going to the middle of nowhere," he replied. "I'm just going to go crazy anyway, so better to do it where I won't kill anyone." Shoulders slumped, he continued on to the truck, got in, and drove away.

Shadow whined and pawed at me. I absently reached a hand down and pet him. Ash was sniffing the bodies, whining a bit herself as she tried to puzzle out what had happened to her friend.

"We should take his advice," Lena said.

I nodded. I didn't have anything left here, myself. There was no reason to stay, so why not go somewhere else? "Want to go back to your village? Check for survivors?"

"Just for a bit," she replied. "After that, let's head south."

I smiled slightly. A bit of warmth to ease the relentless cold sounded nice. "Somewhere where all the snow actually melts in the summer?" I asked. "Sure."

We turned our backs on the bodies and started off toward the train yard, the dogs eventually following after us. We had a long way to go before dark.